A Cali Christmas

by Jenny Dee

A Cali Christmas

©2020 by Jennifer Dee Communications LLC

Art & Photography ©2020 Dusan Petkovic/Depositphotos.com, Darius K./ Depositphotos.com

ISBN: 978-1-7346295-8-3
Printed in the United States of America

Dedication

*For my favorite fellow cheesy cable
Christmas movie junkie, Kristen.
This one's for you, my friend!*

Prologue

December 21, 1999

She stood there at the brink of where the ocean met the sand, longing to freeze time in that very moment; *wishing* she could freeze time in that very moment. She gazed upon the miles and miles of white-capped waves that dove and played, taunting a lone seal who kept losing at hide and seek as the ebbs revealed him.

How she wished she could be that seal. Then nobody would be able to tell her what to do or where to go; she would have the freedom to choose.

Crash went the waves. Screech went the annoying white beach vultures scavenging for crumbs. Louder came the faded giggles of nearby toddlers. Barely audible reggae music escaped a single teen's headphones.

She held tightly on to those sounds, not knowing when she would ever hear that beautiful symphonic clash again. She held on to this little slice of heaven—something that no one could take away from her.

Well, almost no one, she realized, as she screamed out from the ice-cold ocean water that now covered her from head to toes, courtesy of an unexpected pail dumping delivered by her impish companion.

"Grrr, I'm going to get you for this!" she yelled, running as fast as her slender legs could take her toward the laughing scoundrel.

"Not if you can't catch me," he shouted back in glee, pounding his athletic feet into the coarse sand. Unluckily for him, he didn't count on her agility in the sand to catch up, where normally he would have escaped on a flat surface.

Down to the ground they tumbled, twirling around and becoming completely engulfed in the sprinkles of sand that clung to their wet bodies like a poignant memory. Consumed with laughter and revenge, the two duked it out until they finally called a truce and settled into solitude side by side.

The orange-tinted sun was setting way too fast as the shadowy swells furiously crashed upon the cooling beach terrain. The wind was picking up, its presence made known by the chill that followed. Loose tendrils of golden blonde curls danced around young Loralee Cox's pensive baby face as she lay next to her best friend in the whole world, Evan Bosko.

The disappearing light meant that their time together was coming to an end. Tonight was their last night before the Cox family moved across the country to New York City to follow Joselyn Cox's dream of becoming a Broadway star. Unfortunately for these 12-year-old besties, that meant Loralee, along with her little sister, Aimee, had to uproot everything they'd ever known because of their dreamy mother.

Goodbye beautiful Pacific shores of Laguna Beach, and hello cement fields of New York City.

"I wish I didn't have to leave," pouted Loralee, frustrated that her destiny was ruled by a whimsical parent. Since her father had passed away in a car accident two years back, the two sisters were at the mercy of their mother's impulses. Usually it wasn't too bad; a boring party, a new boyfriend or a local theater show she starred in.

But this—leaving their home behind to pursue Joselyn's pipe dreams in a city they'd never even visited before—was more than the eldest daughter could take.

"I know, Ellie," cooed Evan, matching her melancholy. He was the only one who could call her that since her father died; the only one special enough in her eyes to not tarnish that sacred father-daughter nickname. Everyone else was forbidden to do so—especially her family. Evan took great care to only use it when they were alone and out of earshot.

Awkwardly tall and built for his age, the naturally tanned young boy with the long brown tangled surfer hair and Atlantic blue eyes didn't have the right words to offer as comfort. But he did know how to bring the radiant smile back to her sweetheart mouth.

"Come with me," he gestured, taking Loralee by the hand and pulling her toward the end of the beach.

"We'll be back," he shouted over to Mrs. Cox and his mother. Anita Bosko turned her sunglass-covered eyes toward him with a nod of acknowledgment. She was more than happy to dismiss her mopey son so she could enjoy the rest of her time with her friend and their pair of margaritas in silence.

"Where are we going?" inquired the young beauty.

"You'll see," he said with that boyishly handsome grin that made her feel at home. They walked hand-in-hand down the quieting edge of the water, speaking not a single word. A few days before Christmas, beachgoers were already packing up to seek warm refuge in their homes, leaving the stretch of beach before them isolated and private. With their heads hung low, only the surprise of a cold wave hitting their bare feet would jolt them back into reality with a giggle.

Evan led them down to the end of the small family beach, a blockade of large black rocks marking its boundary. Within the puddling waters among the coves were said to be glorious tide pools of marine life at low tide. At a rare moment of perfect timing, Loralee and Evan carefully climbed up and over the rock formations to gaze into the magic that awaited them below.

Colors swirled together as the ecosystem below revealed its secrets. Careful not to disturb the environment, they cautiously sat down upon a large rock to gaze and point at the wonders they saw: a red bat star (which is different from a starfish, Evan explained), a few secluded hermit crabs, several purple sea urchins and a whole bunch of mussels and barnacles. Loralee held her breath as she took it all in.

"I'm certainly not going to see anything like this in New York," she muttered in frustration.

"No, but think of all the wonderful things you *will* be able to see."

"Yeah, like what? Concrete and taxi cabs?"

Evan let out a good-natured laugh at his friend's dramatic sarcasm. It was something he absolutely adored about her, while other girls her age were only interested in trying out their new pre-pubescent flirting techniques. Loralee kept it real, and he liked that.

He hated to see her so down, but somehow, he always had a way of finding the bright side of life; as if he held a magical silver crayon that drew a line around any of Loralee's clouds.

"No. Like the Empire State Building or the Statue of

Liberty. Or Times Square where the ball drops for New Year's. Like South Street Seaport or Chelsea Piers or any of the other exciting landmarks in Manhattan."

"You certainly seem to know a lot about New York City for a little surfer dude," she teased.

"That's because I'm planning on visiting you, and when I do, I want you to be able to take me to the best spots," he announced with confidence.

"Oh, really? Well, how would you ever survive without the ocean?" she jabbed, until she fell into a rare moment of vulnerability while in the comfort of her confidant. "It's the question I keep asking myself," she admitted in a soft voice as she looked out upon the endless miles of ocean once again. It always soothed her so.

"Ellie, there is so much more than just a city there. I heard my mom say that a train to Long Island will have you at a beach in less than 30 minutes. Sure, it may not be the Pacific, but there is still the sun, sand and waves for you to visit."

"It's not the same, Evan," she lamented. "It won't have you."

It was then that she looked up at him with her beachy brown eyes that brimmed with salty tears. For a moment, the two young friends just stood there and looked at each other in the silhouette of the setting sun. Evan had no comeback or silver lining for this one.

But he did know what he needed to do next.

Jumping down off their viewing rock—careful not to rip open his toes on a sharp, protruding edge—Evan began drawing a huge circle in the sand, decorating the outside with seashells and tiny rocks in a holly-like shape.

"What are you doing now?" Loralee asked with a mix of curiosity and irritation. She could tell her mischievous buddy was up to something just by the intensity of his movements. But he refused to answer, lost in his work, while she crossed her arms over her chest and impatiently tapped her foot on the wave-smoothed ledge she still stood upon.

Finally finished with his sand art, he took her by the waist and lifted her down off the precarious boulder. He brought her into the circle with him, holding both of her hands in his and warmly looking right into her eyes.

"Ellie, I will never care about another girl the way I care about you. You are my best friend in the entire world, and I won't say goodbye. I will only say, 'Until later.' We *will* see each other again. I know it. But whenever one of us misses the other, we can draw this mistletoe in the sand and remember this moment; remember *us*."

Evan then closed his eyes and leaned in to gently give Loralee her first kiss—*his* first, too. Sweet, innocent and perfect, like childhood should be. She instinctively closed her eyes, a smile lingering after the tender moment passed. Yes, she would remember this moment forever; the best moment of her entire life.

They then walked back to their mothers, holding hands and uttering not a single sound until they were forced to part ways.

With a warm hug and a final look into each other's youthful eyes, they vowed in unison, "Until later."

1

November 12, 2019

The tiny office space lost within the floors of the tall structure on Park Avenue was bustling with workers running back and forth between meetings and trying to conduct quiet conference calls in open-air cubicles. It was another busy season for LCox Affairs—and November especially brought in the last-minute holiday party planners.

And that meant everyone wanted Loralee's attention, approval—or both.

"Hetherson wants to know if we were able to book the Plaza for his office party," questioned her chunky, lovable red-headed assistant, Caroline.

"Well, did we?" Loralee responded, detesting how it was assumed that she had to make every call and plan every detail. This was her business, true, but wasn't that the whole point of hiring workers—to have people on hand to help her run the show?

Tone down the inner sarcasm, she warned herself, before it leaked out onto her undeserving supporters.

"I—I don't know," Caroline responded with confusion. "Was I supposed to make the call? Usually you are the one to handle our big-name clients."

Loralee sent her trusted right-hand associate one of

her famous forced (but you'd never know it) smiles before responding.

"I think it's time we talked about giving you a bigger role," she answered. "But to put your mind at ease—yes. The Plaza is booked for Friday, December 18th for Mr. Hetherson's party of 20. I've outlined the menu, suggested decorations and recommended live bands as he requested. I put the folder in your mailbox to compile and send over to him for his approval."

Caroline breathed a sigh of relief—until Loralee motioned her into her bright, cheery yellow corner office and beckoned for her assistant to close the door behind her.

Caroline gave the room she so often entered a brief look over. Everything was always in its place—every framed photo, award on display and knickknack that lined her bookshelves; never a dust mite or a single disheveled piece of paper not in its color-coordinated and properly-labeled folder.

And yet, Loralee's office was always warm and welcoming. It must have been the sunshine yellow and subtle beach decorations that hinted at the underbelly of the always-sophisticated professional.

"Is everything okay?" she questioned her boss nervously. She wasn't usually intimidated by Loralee, but she could sense the pressure cooker of stress hidden behind her earlier comments.

"Yes, of course. You are doing a fantastic job as always. But I think it's time for you to do more."

"I already feel a bit overwhelmed right now, Loralee, if I'm being honest. If I took on anymore, my husband would trade me in for a dog."

"I'm aware," Loralee said, trying to suppress a

chuckle. "I wouldn't want Tommy to trade you in—you're too good of a catch. That's why I am arranging for Gloria to take over some of your more administrative duties. Do you think she is ready?"

"I—I guess so." It was obvious that the twenty-something protégé was petrified of what her boss was suggesting. She writhed in her chair—did Loralee misunderstand Caroline's previous assessment of Gloria's capabilities? No, it must just be her nerves.

A lover of herbal tea, Loralee always had an endless supply ready for any of her office guests and offered a soothing cup of honey vanilla chamomile to her grateful employee.

"Caroline, you have been with me the last five years and have done an extraordinary job. But I am overwhelmed myself and could use someone I trust taking over a few of my accounts. Like Hetherson and Danali. I think you are ready for them—and with it comes a raise and a big commission," she added with a wink.

"But—" she started to protest, then reconsidered. "Are you really sure about this?"

"I am. I think you have a wonderfully creative side that you don't get to express often from behind a pile of paperwork. Although Hetherson is pretty much set, I'll leave you to take the final negotiations from here. I also left Danali's blueprint in your mailbox for you to work up your own suggestions for his daughter's Christmas Soirée. You were in on that meeting—I have no doubt you took your own diligent notes and can feel what he is looking for."

Sensing Caroline's hesitation, she knew she had to offer a little more than a bigger paycheck to make the transition easier.

"I'll take a look before you submit the proposal, but I have complete faith in you, Caroline. So much so, that I already told them you were taking over."

"How did you know I would say yes?"

"Because," she began, as she opened the door for her newly promoted employee to exit, "I would have fired you if you didn't." Loralee laughed to release the tension and communicate that she was only joking.

"Go ahead and figure out a game plan on how to transition Gloria, and then we can iron out the details."

Caroline thanked her boss with great appreciation and the spark of joy finally entered the apprentice's eyes as she left the room to take the next step in her career with pride.

Sitting back down at her desk, Loralee felt a sense of relief wash over her. With those two accounts off her caseload, she could focus on the crème de la crème— landing the big Brooks deal. She had followed the annual Holiday Extravaganza for the last ten years, and she finally felt she was in a position to put in a bid and win.

Every year, the famous family hosted a beachside gala for their friends and those acquaintances worthy enough to merit an invitation. No expense was ever spared—and the theme each year had to be something that no one else could ever match.

Word on the street was that Thatcher Brooks was tired of the same old companies vying for the job and wanted to broaden his horizons to seek out "new blood." One more trite "winter wonderland" and he'd jump right into an ocean of sharks.

To say that Loralee was surprised that a personal request from Mr. Brooks himself came across her inbox was an understatement.

Your work is held in high regard by one of my most
respected colleagues. I do hope you will consider submitting
a bid this year. I look forward to your proposal.

She couldn't help but shout out in girlish jubilee that Thatcher Brooks had reached out to her—some small event planner in a sea of many in New York City. Almost all her staff came running toward her office to see what the commotion was all about—only to be warned that they needed to be on top of their game this year; that there was no room for error on even the tiniest event.

It was unusual for her to push any of her loyal customers to the side; but that day, she needed to seize the opportunity and put her whole heart into a winning proposal. There wasn't a detail she'd missed—except for the theme.

She diplomatically phrased its omittance, citing this was something she could not do until she could personally speak to Mr. Brooks and learn more about him and the event. To present an idea without that kind of background would make it sterile and cookie-cutter, and she prided herself on designing parties that were customized to the personalities of her clients.

It was a huge risk she was taking; but even as much as she wanted this account, she was not going to compromise her standards or reputation just to answer a bid question. She had hoped with all her being that her integrity could sell her the business.

Landing the Brooks account would be a dream come true for her—and an explosion for her business if executed perfectly. Of course, aside from the notoriety she'd gain, she felt pulled by the mere thought of the extravaganza being held in her childhood hometown: Laguna Beach, California. A place she had long left behind.

Twenty years had passed since she last saw her beloved childhood home. It seemed like a lifetime ago. She barely remembered what her house looked like, or the names of the kids who played on her street, or the sights and sounds of her beloved beach she tried so hard to burn into her memory that final night.

Or Evan Bosko. She could never truly forget him, though time had its way of fading him out with each passing year like an old polaroid.

If only they had the technology twenty years ago that they had today, it would have been much easier for them to keep in touch.

For the first few years, Loralee and Evan wrote long, weekly letters to each other. Oh, how she would look forward to running to the mailbox every Friday to find his letter waiting for her. And then she would spend her Friday night huddled in the corner of whatever private space she could find, spilling her heart out on endless streams of paper for the mailman to send back the next morning.

Every letter revealed a new adventure for him. He was practicing his surfing and getting better every day. His dad also let him start helping out on their family boat, so he was learning all about navigating the bumpy seas. He said he was going to use that knowledge to go find some buried treasure and live life like a pirate. *Typical Evan,* she'd muse.

He'd go on and on about all their friends at school and the latest art festivals or beach parties. Loralee would close her eyes and imagine being back in that place, listening to the music and swaying, or staring at a weird, yet interesting piece of artwork on display. Sometimes, Evan would send her some printed pictures so she could feel like she was there. Oh, how it would make her miss her home even more.

Loralee would confide in him about the miserable little apartments she lived in, the urine-soaked, stinky streets and some mean kids at school. She'd tell him about her mother's latest failed theater gig or how Loralee learned to cook for the family—otherwise they'd never eat a proper dinner.

She didn't have an easy time adjusting to her new life but had found solace in coloring and drawing. They lived within walking distance of Central Park at one point, where she would sneak out early in the morning to catch the sunrise and all of its colors. She sent some of her drawings to Evan, who would rave about them in his next letter.

Art was the only joy that brought a smile to Loralee's face—except hearing from Evan. He'd somehow continue to draw that silver lining for her and lift her spirits every time. Whenever she was particularly down, he'd send a photo of a beach mistletoe he had made for her to remind her of their special night.

And each letter would always end the same: "Until later." Holding on to the thought of seeing him again got Loralee through many challenging times.

But as the years went by and her mother moved their family from place to place—including a few homeless shelters—Loralee had soon lost her treasured letters, her cherished photos and any means of contacting Evan. She frantically searched and searched for that tiny piece of paper she tore off the corner of an envelope so she would have his latest address. But one day, it had just vanished, along with her shoebox of memories, and her world came crashing down around her then 16-year-old life.

Why couldn't I just remember his address? she chided herself, as if wishing for it would make it appear.

He probably thought she forgot all about him; wondered why one day she just never wrote him again. Her heart became a mosaic of shattered glass over the thought of how hurt he must have felt. How lost she was going to be without her best friend in the whole world.

By the time she was old enough to afford technology or use social media, Loralee was way too busy to track anyone down; not even her first kiss. It was mostly shame and pride that kept her from reaching out. How could she ever explain how her life crashed and burned?

Needless to say, Joselyn never hit it big on Broadway. Her mother pounced from waitressing gig to bartending job to whatever side hustle she could find while Loralee was left to raise her little sister. Life was no longer the privileged existence she remembered of the shores along the Pacific Coast Highway when her Daddy was alive.

No, it became a hard-knock life that Loralee needed to rise above—and she did, thanks to her exemplary academic brain winning her the much-needed full scholarships to college. Loralee put all of her energy into excelling in school so that she could start her own business after she graduated. She was determined to take charge of her own destiny, and that included financial freedom.

To help pay for books and supplies, she worked for a party planner and immediately fell in love with the industry. She knew that one day, she would be the one organizing grand events and bringing joy into people's lives. She lit up at the thought of a life purpose.

And now, she was living her dream. LCox Affairs was her pride and joy, built from countless hours of blood, sweat and tears.

By the time college came, thankfully, Joselyn had humbled from life and became the mother she needed to be for Aimee, and for Loralee. Now, the three of them were closer than ever. Joselyn was an acclaimed hairdresser, sought out by well-to-do corporate types. She dated once in a while but seemed content to finally be on her own and excelling in her new calling.

In fact, it was Joselyn's new connections that helped to quickly spread the word around about Loralee's party planning business. With that kind of publicity, it didn't take long for Loralee to make a solid name for herself.

Aimee eventually went to school to become a veterinarian's assistant, where she met and married Daniel Moringuez—after rescuing his bulldog, Rocky, from a thorn in the paw. It was love at first sight for the two, and the entire family loved and respected the hardworking family man. He was perfect for sweet, gentle Aimee.

Their family grew with the addition of two boisterous boys, Joey and Mitch, who brought such joy to the family with their diverse interests: one an athletic soccer star and the other a guitar-playing protégé. How Loralee adored those boys, since she didn't have any children of her own.

Loralee herself dated on occasion but could never quite find the time to concentrate on nurturing a relationship. It was a goal she had for herself when business settled down and she had a few account executives she could count on. She did want that love and a family of her own one day. It just wasn't in the cards for her right now—especially not with the Brooks account looming over her head.

Knowing this opportunity was in front of her made Loralee remember all that she lost and loved back in California. It brought back so many questions she tried not to think about.

Why hadn't she gone back there in all these years, even for a visit? Did it still look the same as she remembered? Why hadn't Evan tried to track *her* down?

But she couldn't drift off into memory lane right now. Odds were that Evan was married with a handful of kids by now—or a bachelor with a string of pretty women serving him beers beachside on his private pirate island. At the mention of her name, he'd probably wonder, "Loralee who?"

Surprised by how long the thought of Evan lingered in her reverie, she shook the thoughts aside to bring her attention back to her business. She had a few loose ends to tie up before she'd be done for the day. She hadn't expected to hear a decision back from Brooks for another day or two, but she optimistically prepared for a life-changing announcement regardless.

All other clients had to be personally checked in with and assured, because if that miracle happened, she'd be thrown into a whirlwind of busy that would otherwise jeopardize her foundation if she hadn't given them the attention they deserved.

After a few hours of phone calls and email verifications, Loralee was ready to call it a night and head home to her tiny but comfortable one-bedroom apartment in Greenwich Village. A night of takeout, wine and some terrible reality television saved on her DVR was the perfect way to end her busy day.

The following morning, she walked in to see her office workers all abuzz and staring at her. *Did I have a piece of spinach stuck in my teeth from my morning omelet?* she wondered as she subtly tried to feel around her teeth with her tongue.

"What's going on?" she asked, flagging down a flustered Caroline, dressed in a beautiful black and white checkered suit, Loralee noticed. It warmed her heart to see the professionalism that soared in her former assistant. She had made the right choice to promote her for certain.

"Loralee, you are not going to believe this," Caroline exclaimed, excitedly out of breath. "We just got the call—you're in! Brooks picked you for this year's Holiday Extravaganza!"

2

Loralee's heart stopped. She felt like she needed to pinch herself—did she just hear Caroline correctly? Brooks picked *her?*

"Well, aren't you going to say anything?" prompted Caroline.

"I—I'm at a loss for words," Loralee barely managed.

"That's a first," she teased. Collecting her bearings, Loralee looked around to see the entire office at attention, carefully watching her with smiles of support. The whole room was lit up with the warmth and affection of a team she had treated well for so many years.

"I can't believe this is really happening. I—I have to thank you all for everything you have done for me to make LCox Affairs worthy of such an honor. I couldn't have done it without you." Cheers and applause broke out before everyone scurried back to their desks—Loralee didn't have to tell them what landing this account meant.

Extra diligence with their existing clientele and all hands on deck was needed to make sure this Holiday Extravaganza went off without a hitch. It could be the coup that could land LCox as the leading event planner in New York City—and possibly, in California as well.

Yet, Loralee continued to stand in the center of the office, unusually frazzled and uncertain of what to do next. She had hoped this would happen, but now that it has, she knew a lot was on the line: her reputation, her life's work and the return to a childhood town she had left behind.

"Loralee, how can I help?" quietly quizzed Caroline, who had noticed her boss' frozen state and gently guided her toward her office for privacy.

"I'm overwhelmed. Excited, but overwhelmed. I don't know where to start."

"I figured you might be a little shell-shocked by the news, so I started a file for you. After the call, Brooks' assistant, Christy, followed up with an email outlining our next steps. Legal is drawing up a contract, so first we should review their terms and make sure you can meet their expectations."

Grateful to have someone leading the organizational charge, Loralee was starting to readjust to reality and find her groove again. She was ready to get down to business.

"Anything in there I might object to?"

"Looks pretty standard. Except Brooks expects you to be in California soon, and for the duration of the weeks leading up to the extravaganza. That means you won't be home for Thanksgiving."

"I can appreciate Brooks wanting my undivided attention, especially when he is taking such a big risk on a local out-of-towner. I'm sure my family will understand. Anything else?"

"No, but it looks like you will be pretty well taken care of. He had Christy already send over suggested flight information and hotel recommendations. We just have to let her know your preferences and she will take care of the rest."

"Okay, great. I'll take a look at this now and get back to her today. Thank you, Caroline. I don't know what I would do without you."

"And you never have to, boss. I'm all in. Anything you need, I will make it happen. Your success is my success. And you are going to do an absolutely amazing job. I just know it."

Loralee smiled as her trusted friend left the office to give her time to sort through the details.

There was so much to take in and it was happening so fast. She essentially had a week to put her affairs in order before flying out to live in California for the next month. She got straight to work, first on highlighting any changes to the contract, and second on selecting her flights and accommodations.

Once that was taken care of, she called her mother and sister to arrange for dinner that night so she could share her good news with them.

"So, what's this big dinner all about? It's not like you to be finished with work so early on a weekday evening— especially so close to the holidays," Joselyn keenly observed with motherly intuition.

"Well," her proud daughter responded, pouring her mother and sister each a glass of Cabernet, "do you remember how I told you I was putting in a proposal for Thatcher Brooks' annual holiday event?" She couldn't help but smile so big, the secret revealed itself.

"No!" Aimee squealed with excited delight. "Tell me he picked you!"

"He picked me," she announced with glee.

"Oh honey, that is such wonderful news. Congratulations!"

"Thanks, Mom. It all seems so surreal. First, even getting an invitation to bid and then actually landing the account. I still feel like I'm in a dream."

"Well, you deserve it, Lor. You have worked so hard all these years. This could be your big break, and I couldn't be happier for you," Aimee said as she enveloped her big sister in a loving hug.

"To LCox Affairs and its sensational owner," Joselyn said, raising her glass. "May this change your life in all the best ways." A clinking of the glasses cinched the toast.

"So, what's next? I'm guessing you have to fly out there?" asked Aimee.

"Yeah, that's the other thing I needed to tell you. Brooks needs me to fly out next week and stay for the month until the event is over. I hate to leave you both like this, but it's important that I be there."

"Oh honey, we completely understand. Don't you worry about us. Thanksgiving is at my house this year, and well, you know how I end up ruining the turkey and ordering in anyway. Go and chase those dreams. We'll be here waiting for you for Christmas," Joselyn reassured her. "You will be home for Christmas though, right?"

"Oh yes," Loralee laughed at her mother's not-so-subtle hint. "The event is two weeks before, so I will be home in plenty of time for our annual cookie baking and tree trimming traditions. I wouldn't miss it for the world."

"So, are you nervous about going back to California after all this time?" Aimee inquired.

"Not really. Why should I be?"

"I just know that it was hard on you when we left. You know, there were people there that you were close to and kept in touch with for a while. I was just wondering if you had planned on looking them up when you got there."

"I won't have time to reconnect with old friends, who probably don't even remember me, Aimes," she replied forlornly, trying hard not to let her mind wander over to a forgotten promise. "It's just best to leave it all in the past. My life is here now, and I made peace with that a long time ago. But I will admit, I am looking forward to spending some time at the beach again."

"Oh, that's right!" exclaimed Joselyn. "While we're here avoiding snowstorms, you'll be in sunshine heaven. I almost forgot how wonderful those balmy holidays were. You are one lucky girl, Loralee Cox. I'm so proud of both my girls."

A group hug cemented the love and togetherness the women felt for each other. They had certainly come a long way from childhood chaos, and Loralee couldn't have been happier about life in that very moment.

The rest of her week was consumed with brainstorming, assuring clients and packing. Loralee conducted all the research she possibly could on past extravaganzas—the themes, the locations, the attendees, the reviews. Pages of paperwork were piling up on the printer. It would be a long 6-hour flight, and she would spend the majority of it working on a well-developed PowerPoint game plan.

She personally called each and every client to share her news, and not a single one begrudged her for shifting her focus to this important new opportunity. She was touched by the outpouring of support, each wishing her well in her endeavors and assuring her that they were as confident as she was in their newly appointed LCox account executives. Caroline and team had already reached out to begin the transition and had put everyone at ease that their own events would be masterfully executed as always.

Several transitional meetings were held with Loralee's

team, where she authoritatively turned over control of her company to Caroline in her absence. She had no doubt that the new leader already had the respect of her peers and would encourage a culture of customer-focus and productivity. Loralee had no qualms of leaving her only child in someone else's capable hands.

Yet, on her last day in the office, she couldn't help but be an overprotective mama bear, making sure every last detail was in order. Caroline and Gloria were subjected to one final meeting before Loralee would breathe a sigh of relief and relinquish complete control to her confidants.

"Remind me again where we are with Hetherson?"

"Hetherson just confirmed anticipated guest counts yesterday, so that is set. Contracts with all vendors are signed, and Gloria followed up with the florist, band, chocolate fountain machine rental, caterer, linens and decorator this morning. There is literally nothing else we can do except follow up over the next two weeks to make sure all orders are placed and that there have been no last-minute changes."

"Perfect, thank you. And Danali—what's the status with that?"

"We have a meeting on Tuesday to discuss the menu. He has a few adjustments he'd like to make to the appetizer selections, but nothing the caterer can't handle. Same as Henderson, everything else is set," Gloria chimed in, feeling comfortable in her new role as executive assistant. Loralee had made another good choice in promoting a loyal and competent employee.

"And what about—"

"Loralee," Caroline cut her off with a reassuring smile. "Let me save you some trouble. Donovan signed off this morning on the reindeer theme, so we are working on some of the ideas you gathered last week for it. We have a call this afternoon to go through them, and then we will take it from there. Contracts will be signed for Ellis by Monday. Tonag, Flinns, Austin, Redisson and Galla are all set. I promise you, if we run into any issues, I will call you."

"I know, I'm sorry. I know you have everything under control and not a single detail will get by either of you. I guess I am just more nervous about this trip than I realized," Loralee explained as she began to pace back and forth.

"Is there anything else we can do to help?" asked Gloria.

"No, but thank you. I appreciate all your hard work. I promise that there will be an extra-special Christmas bonus waiting for the both of you," she smiled in response.

"I do it because I love what I do, Miss Cox. But thank you," Gloria replied with sincerity as she excused herself for lunch. Caroline hung back for a few extra minutes to make sure her boss' mind was truly put at ease.

"Loralee, forgive me for saying this, but you seem a little more apprehensive than you usually are. I know that you are confident in our abilities and have checked all of these details yourself already. Is there something else bothering you?"

Loralee gazed out of her corner office window into the busy streets of New York. The concrete home she resisted but had become so accustomed to; the speed of which helped her to forget her past and look toward an exciting future. She had lied to Aimee about how poignant this trip to California would be for her. She wasn't sure she could repress it any longer.

"Actually, do you have a minute?"

"Of course, Loralee. What's wrong?"

"I'm nervous about going to California. But not because of this account. I have enough faith in myself to know that I wouldn't have been selected if Brooks didn't already do his homework and know what I brought to the table."

"Then what is it?"

"Growing up in Laguna Beach—you can see just by looking around my office how much it meant to me," she began, turning to face her friend with rare tears forming in her eyes. "I have fought so hard to forget all about that place. And now the thought of returning—it's unsettling."

"But why? I thought you had so many happy memories there."

"That's just it. I did. But I had put them behind me. I'm not sure if I am ready for my past to resurface." She spoke quietly, barely above a whisper as she finally confided what was plaguing her heart.

"Are we talking about a place—or a person?" Caroline probed gently.

"Both, I guess. Caroline, it's where I was born. Where I lived with my dad until he died. Everything I remember about him lives there, including how his death left Aimee and me with an erratic mother. I'd run to the ocean for solace and find my sanity in a grain of beach sand.

"It's where I had my first kiss, and where I left a childhood love behind. Friends and school and art festivals and this freedom to be a child. It's just so full of memories—both happy and sad—that I'm not sure if I will be able to contain myself professionally if they all come rushing back to me."

"I see," she responded delicately. "So, you are afraid that emotions you had buried long ago will surface and throw you off balance? Ruin your chances with Brooks?"

"In a sense, yes," she admitted with relief, glad to finally have purged what she was holding within to someone who evidently grasped what she was feeling.

"Oh Loralee, you are one of the most put together, polished professionals I know. Even if sitting on the beach brings you back to sadder times, I know you would never let that interfere with your work. You are too sensible and dedicated to jeopardize all you have worked for. There's nothing for you to worry about."

"In my head, I know that. But I haven't let myself remember my life in Laguna for a very long time. This is different, Caroline. I—I don't know what to expect, and it's stirring up all of these emotions inside me already. I just don't want to blow this opportunity."

"Perhaps you should push off your initial meeting with Brooks for a few days so you can confront what is waiting for you in Laguna first," she offered as advice, wanting more than anything to soothe her friend's nerves. "Then maybe you will realize that all this anxiety you built up is mostly in your head, and you can let go and focus on the task at hand. But give yourself that time and space first. Don't ignore it; feel it and then move on."

Loralee's eyes swelled at the wisdom and kindness in Caroline's words. She had an excellent point; she needed a day or two to adjust to her surroundings before they got the better of her. It wouldn't do her any good to pretend that this trip was like any other. A few days at her beloved beach reconciling her memories sounded like exactly what she needed before getting down to business.

"That sounds like a great idea. Thank you," replied Loralee in gratitude. "Would you mind making the arrangements to postpone the meeting for me? I'm sure he will understand that I will have some personal business to attend to first, as well as wanting to get rid of the jet lag before giving him my undivided attention."

"Of course, my friend. I'll get right on it and send you a confirmation," she affirmed, bobbing her way out of the office. "Loralee—if you need me at all while you are away, please remember I am here for you. You don't have to go through this alone."

Loralee smiled as she exited, then simply sat there in her office, staring at the beach artwork she had hanging on her brightly colored wall. Soon that image would be her reality, and there was only one thing left for her to do.

Pack her final bags and get ready to leave with unprecedented butterflies in her stomach.

3

All the way to the airport, nerves plagued Loralee as she went through the tedious check-in and security process and then anxiously awaited her boarding call. Out of habit, she checked her email several times, as well as texted Caroline twice before turning off her phone to concentrate on anything but the feelings that were stirring inside.

In six hours, she would be landing at Long Beach airport, a mere forty-five minutes away from her native hometown. She wondered what the artsy little village would be like when she arrived after twenty years of her absence. Would anything look the same or would everything be unfamiliar as if she were exploring a brand-new place? That particular thought put her mind at ease— after all, if nothing remained the same, then the memories couldn't come back to haunt her.

How much of her old stomping grounds should she visit? She had to admit, curiosity ran wild about what her childhood home looked like now, who was living in her old neighborhood and if the Sawdust Festival she loved to walk through as a child was still going strong.

She recalled the many artistic booths that inspired her creative drawings, envisioning that one day she would grow up to have a booth there that visitors would marvel at. One of her framed masterpieces could even make it onto a wall in someone's home as a discussion piece for guests.

Would she recognize any of those old beach cottages viewable from the main Pacific Coast Highway, or would modernization have touched them by now and taken away their antique charm?

Speaking of antiques, she pondered if the vintage shop owned by the kind old Guadalupe Rivera was still in business—that is, if his son Felipe took over ownership or if someone else bought the place and preserved its authenticity.

She noticed in her research that they offered a historic tour of the town, piquing her interest to see what old gems might still be intact versus what remodeling had occurred. Do those open-aired, red trolleys still transport people to and from the different main street hot spots?

Nostalgia overtook her as she dreamily walked through the gate to board the plane. She'd find out soon enough how much has changed—or remained the same— since she was a young girl.

For now, she had to spend the next few hours focused on a game plan. Appreciatively, Thatcher Brooks arranged for Loralee to travel in style via first class, giving her the luxury of space and a sophisticated row mate to spend the trip with; one who fell asleep quickly without snoring and left her to her mental work in peace.

She thought about her newest client and how she was already at ease with the man. A few brief, preliminary phone calls revealed his deep, gruff voice and hearty, booming laugh—which he gifted to listeners frequently with his somewhat politically incorrect sense of humor. His mannerisms made her feel like Brooks was more easygoing than she would have anticipated a rich west coaster with high expectations to be.

She hoped that she liked him in person as much as she already respected him on the phone. It would make working with him and extracting his ideas much easier than having to guess what he was looking for in a grand holiday event.

Loralee spent the entire plane ride reading up on Brooks to see if she could glean anything personal from which to build a theme idea. It was the one thing he had tasked her with working on—he was appreciative of the fact that she didn't want to be cookie-cutter, but since he was taking a risk, he was clear that pursuing this partnership would mean securing an approved theme almost instantaneously.

He not-so-subtly hinted that if it didn't work out, he had another, more experienced vendor waiting in the wings. So, as lenient as he was, he was still a businessman who expected results. And Loralee Cox was determined to deliver.

After culling through all the research that she had printed out, and highlighting what worked and what didn't work in the past, she started outlining some new ideas she could bring to the table. She concurred that the winter wonderland theme was way overdone. Secret Santas, white elephant exchanges and grab bags were also a tad obsolete. So far, all she could find was what she wouldn't be suggesting this year.

Come on, Loralee, you've been doing this for over ten years. Surely, there is something you have done that might be original enough to please Thatcher Brooks, she begged her mind archives to reveal.

Ah, yes. There was this "Candy Cane Lane" event that Hetherson once raved about. It was actually set up much like the child's game—a la Willy Wonka style—with oversized candy canes lining the entranceway, trees trimmed entirely of candy canes and lollipops and secret candy grams with holiday wishes written to fellow employees.

It really was a fantastic event, though a lot of those attendees were family-based. She wasn't sure how well this idea would go over in a more upscale crowd at the Brooks Holiday Extravaganza. But, satisfied that she had an idea to start with, Loralee jotted down some preliminary concepts that could work for the elegant affair.

Then, she thought back to the time LCox built an indoor snow stadium, where guests could play in snow pits to build snowmen and even slide down ice mountains. *Hmm, too much like the old winter wonderland theme,* she reminded herself. *Scratch that one.*

The current reindeer idea she developed for the Donovan account might be clever—and in California, thanks to the nice weather, she could bring in horses and dress them up like reindeer and have them draw carriages for an extra touch. O*r maybe that would be deemed animal cruelty,* she surmised and noted the idea as tentative.

Well, whatever the theme ended up being, she did like the notion of incorporating horse-drawn sleighs into the plan and thought she would at least present it as an option.

Oh, that's been done, she noted dejectedly as she came across a past "Santa's Sleigh" theme Brooks hosted about five years ago. Still—there was something tugging at her that she could reinvent this idea into something a little different. She placed a sticky note on the page to remind her to come back and brainstorm this again after the theme was set.

This is going to be harder than I thought, she

considered. *What do I know about Thatcher Brooks?*

Loralee knew he was a self-made millionaire, who built his fortune from the ground up as a real estate investor—basically through what one would call "flipping houses" today. He was a master of turning beaten-down buildings with old school charm into breathtaking historical refurbishments.

He still lived with his wife, Veronica, in their secluded Irvine Beach community located right on the Pacific Ocean beachfront, said to mimic a private resort. She selfishly wondered if she could earn herself an invite to their exquisite home to see what a day in the life of the insanely wealthy was like. Although, she was certain it had been quite lonely since their only daughter, Isabella, died tragically a few years back from stage four breast cancer. She was saddened to read about that heartbreak in his profile.

One of his favorite pastimes was golf, of course— *hmm, what if she created a hole-in-one mini golf setup, with each station having its own Christmas theme?* Now that was something that no one had thought about before! That idea quickly rose to the top of her suggestion list.

Satisfied that she had spent more than half the flight coming up with solid brainstorms, Loralee allowed herself to rest into a peaceful slumber before facing her destination with trepidation.

The warmth of the November air surprised her as she stepped out of the plane and into the outdoors. Unusual, she thought, as she was used to deboarding into a temporary tunnel that encased passengers indoors on their way back to the airport building. Here, she walked down a set of stairs to the actual landing area and then walked around a designated pathway before briefly entering a small building, which only led to another outdoor area for baggage claim.

I'm certainly not in New York anymore, she chuckled to herself.

Knowing it would take a while for the baggage to unload, she treated herself to a cool caramel Frappuccino before making her way toward baggage claim number two, which was also housing three other arriving flights.

She was already apprehensive about arriving on California soil as it was, and just wanted to get to her hotel to regroup—but now she had to worry about where her bag ended up in the mix of multiple airlines. She'd have to keep a close eye out so she could grab it and run to avoid the crowds.

While waiting, she checked her phone to see the incoming text from her shuttle service confirming her pickup in fifteen minutes, along with a few comforting messages from Caroline that everything was just fine and one from her mother with a reminder to let her know when she landed.

Deciding to pick up the phone and put her mother at ease with her voice, Loralee thought it might be a good way to pass the time while impatiently waiting for her luggage to arrive on the slow carousel.

"Hey baby girl, so good to hear your voice. How was the flight?"

"Not too bad. I was able to get a lot of work done and take a nap. Just waiting here at the baggage claim and then I'll be off to my hotel."

"How's the weather there?"

"A temperate seventy degrees," she smirked, not

wanting to rub it in Joselyn's face.

"I'm so jealous," Joselyn whined. "Don't forget to stop by a souvenir shop to see if you can bring me home a new Greeter statue. I wonder if it is still up in the center of town?"

Loralee noticed her bag starting to emerge out of the corner of her eye, indicating it was time to go.

"I promise I'll check it out. Mom, I've got to go, my bag is here." Getting Joselyn to hang up the phone was sometimes a chore—and Loralee hoped that she could catch her bag before it got sucked back into another lengthy conveyor rotation.

"Okay, Lor, call me—"

"Mom, really, I have to go. I love you, bye." She quickly hung up the phone and made her way over to the carousel, but was pushed aside by a man who towered over her by a good three to four inches, who was reaching for her very bag.

"Excuse me, but that's my bag," she said as she tried to force her way in to stop the man from claiming what wasn't his.

"Nah, I'm pretty sure this is my bag," he responded in a cool, aloof fashion, not turning around to even look at her. He continued to pull it off the belt without so much as looking at the tag to verify ownership.

"Um, no. That would be *my* bag. Unless you have a habit of intertwining red and green ribbon around the handle as an indicator it was *your* bag?"

The tall stranger placed the oversized red suitcase on the ground, noted the very ribbon she described and took a step back.

"Ah, perhaps I was mistaken. My bad," he said as he turned and gave her a goofy, idiotic playboy smile.

A smile that revealed a mouth full of bright white teeth that shone brighter because of his deepened, sun-kissed tan. But that natural-looking charm was not going to win her over to his good graces, she knew that much. In fact, it did the opposite—it irritated her and brought out her overtired, anxious, poor-mannered emotions that were triggered by the sudden change in season and all-too-familiar scenery.

"Maybe you should pay more attention to things like ribbons and this very clearly written luggage tag before assuming something is yours."

"Hey, take it easy. It was an honest mistake. No harm, no foul, girl," he gestured with his hands up, backing away as if his legs drawled along with his words.

Oh, Loralee did not like his flippant attitude and the fact that he had just belittled her into "girl" status when clearly, she was a professional, accomplished woman of her times. Who did this character think he was? And why was he still holding onto *her* bag?

"Excuse me, but I'll be taking that now, sir, if you would get your hands off my bag."

"Wow, someone must have had a rough flight," he continued in his laid-back tone. "Chill out, will ya?" he advised, looking the young, beautiful but tough woman up and down with awe. He decided instantly that she was cute and feisty, very unlike the other women he was accustomed to meeting and avoiding in this affluent little county. He playfully held onto her bag and dared to catch a glimpse of the tag—after all, he figured he had to find out who this wound-up little thing was.

The man was stunned into silence as recognition seeped through his pores. Loralee Cox. He knew that name. The name of someone he once cared about long ago. Renewed in his interest of the woman before him, he slowly looked up, hoping that he wouldn't give away the fact that he once knew her.

And yet, now studying her, how could he not remember? Sure, her once bleach blonde locks gave way to a lighter caramel color with fake salon-created highlights. Her wintery skin was much fairer, but her stature was still short and lean. He bet she could still kick his ass in a beach race, though, he mused.

Those fuller, pink-glossed lips were not as he remembered them, nor was the womanly shape of her grownup body—but he'd never forget those eyes. Time and circumstance may have hardened them, he considered sadly, but the contradicting fire and sweetness that he'd burned into his memory was still very much alive in the flecks of green that stared him down in exasperation.

Ellie.

After all these years, Evan Bosko was standing face-to-face with his first love, and she didn't even have a clue. Judging by her hostility toward him, New York had darkened her demeanor and he wasn't sure he wanted to reveal himself to her just yet.

"Hello? Did you not hear me? Get your damn hands off my bag so I can be on my way," she demanded impatiently.

"God, you must be from New York," he said accusingly, with a hint of teasing. It entertained him to ruffle the feathers of an uptight east coaster—especially one who came back home with a clear chip on her shoulder. Yeah, he was going to wait a while and let this play out. He already knew this wouldn't be the last time their paths would cross, so he chose to keep that secret mum for now and enjoy the mystery.

"And *you* must be a local," she shot back in disdain before walking away and recalling how annoyingly entitled and overly casual the people around here could be. It was coming back to her: the slower pace, the relaxed attitudes, the high on pot mentality. She was undoubtedly a fish out of water after twenty years of fast-paced city street life.

She acknowledged that she needed a drink to calm herself once she got to the hotel, especially if she was already so out of sorts just getting off the plane and engaging in a silly tiff over a piece of luggage. She feared how else she could be easily triggered being back where it all started and took a deep breath to remind herself that everything was going to be okay.

She just needed to get out of this crowded airport and settled into her quiet, cushy hotel room with a martini menu and room service dinner. The thought of having an ocean view room overlooking the Pacific already had the intended soothing effect on her soul. In a few minutes, this would all be behind her and she could begin her journey to executing the most successful event she's ever managed.

Reminding herself of why she was here in the first place, Loralee turned for a moment to give the stranger one last look of disgust before rolling her suitcase triumphantly away. She didn't understand his sudden change in demeanor; the way he looked at her with this familiar longing that seemed odd after such a combative encounter.

That didn't matter, she hissed to herself. His jagged features, sharp jawline and mesmerizing blue eyes were not going to charm her into apologizing or calming down, as he rudely recommended. Not even the already fading memory of his clean-shaven beard stubble that contrasted with his tousled coffee-colored hair and his surfer boy toned body would beat down her weak-kneed defenses.

No, ma'am, she was going to take her luggage and defiantly run far away toward the shuttle service and never look back. The beach would soothe her soul, as it had so many years ago. The sooner she could get to it, the better.

Though she could still feel the burn of his captivated eyes as he amusingly watched her walk away in a typical New Yorker huff.

4

Rattled from baggage claim mayhem and the infamous L.A. traffic (which somehow carried through multiple California counties), Loralee never felt so relieved to fall onto a plush King-sized bed in her entire life. She kicked off her red pumps, unbuttoned her matching blazer and grabbed the hotel's information binder to immediately order something to eat.

She was absolutely starving; and being "hangry" on top of already moody was not the way she wanted to start off this trip. Satisfied with the Surf and Sand Resort's selection of seared scallops and a summer sangria, she allowed the meal to unwind her mind as she sat on her open-door balcony and watched the waves roll in, a mere twenty-five feet away.

As they washed on and off the shore, she was immediately transported back to a summer memory of when her father had rented a small bungalow for her family of four near San Diego for an overnight destination at the beach. They were so excited to sit in a little house and watch the waves dance back and forth in front of the porch. Aimee and Loralee ran down to the beckoning ocean barefoot in the sand, playing truth or dare with the water to see if that threatening wave would reach them whenever it crashed upon the smooth sand.

One such surge caught Aimee and Loralee off-guard,

and their frilly matching yellow daisy sundresses were soaked with the salty water. She could still hear the belly-deep laughter emerging from their father, who found such pure joy in the little moments. Their mother, however, spoiled the fun with her shrieking about how their dresses were ruined and they had no change of clothes. But Logan Cox had a way of melting Joselyn's dramatic heart, and one kiss and twirl in the sand was all it took to convince her to join in on the laughter.

Remembering such a powerful memory brought droplets to her tired eyes. How she longed so many times for her family life to return to such a state of bliss. Her father's death had devastated all of them, but Joselyn lost her way and there was nothing Loralee could do to fill the void left by such a wonderful man. The only comfort Loralee felt after his death was in the time she spent alongside Evan Bosko.

Just saying his name in her head made her heart churn. How after so many years she could still think of him with such fondness and heartache was unimaginable. It was only a first kiss, and a farewell one at that, she reminded herself.

Though trying to convince herself that he didn't matter as much as she thought he did, it didn't stop the wistful desire to somehow find him while she was here.

What was life like for him? He was probably married with tons of children by now. Teaching his own boys how to surf, no doubt. Would he even remember who she was? After all, it was she who ended the communication after she lost his address and moved somewhere he could no longer find her.

But she did not want the sorrow to overtake her. This trip was about bettering her future, not digging up the past. It wouldn't do her any good to try to find out what happened to Evan or force her way into his settled life just because she finally returned after two decades.

No, it was best to let the memories wash out to sea with those of her long-lost father. And it was with thoughts of her two favorite men from youth that Loralee quickly fell into a deep slumber.

Evan sat serenely by the gas-lit fireplace in his suite-like bedroom that overlooked the ocean. The sky was fantastically bright with stars, reflecting off the water in beams of dancing lights. Yet, they held no interest for the man, who was otherwise distracted by an old photo he held in his hand.

A photo of him and Ellie from the last night they were together before her mother whisked her off to New York, never to be seen again. Alongside it, a faded, torn piece of paper housing the drawing she had once made for him of a mistletoe in the sand.

Sighing, Evan tried to make sense of all that had happened since the night he drew her that first beach mistletoe and experienced his first kiss. Their only kiss. And after years of girlfriends and even a beautiful, loving wife who he adored, it was still the only kiss that incited his very soul.

He never thought he would ever see her again after they lost touch—after she stopped responding to his letters. He wrote for months, waiting for any sign from her, until he received a returned letter stating her address was no longer valid. How utterly crushed he was. The light in his life had disappeared, and he didn't know where to find it; find *her.*

Sure, as an adult, he could have done the research. It wouldn't have been difficult to look up the maiden Loralee Cox, especially since she owned her own successful business in Manhattan. He'd been to New York a few times on behalf of his father-in-law's business, but being a happily married man, he thought it would be disloyal to look up a pre-teen flame, and so he never sought Loralee out.

But Thatcher Brooks did, and now Loralee was back in his life.

He wasn't sure how he felt about that. Seeing and fighting with her at the airport was not something he ever expected. Once he saw her name, he was transported to that night and sensed the age-old magic come back to life. He wasn't certain he actually liked the woman she turned out to be, all haughty and full of herself, but he couldn't deny that it stirred him up—but in a much different way than he was stirred up as a 12-year-old.

"What I am going to do about you?" he asked the young girl in the picture before tucking her away in his weathered photo album and turning in for a restless night plagued with dreams of adolescent love.

Loralee woke up the next morning feeling much more refreshed and in control of her emotions. She had another two days before she had to meet with Brooks, so she thought that she'd take advantage of her energized state and reacquaint herself with her old stomping ground.

She started with a simple walk out onto the main highway, which was already bustling with tourists and locals; surprisingly crowded for a random Tuesday morning. The artistic electricity was still in the air and the eclecticism of the storefronts had not changed—modernized, yes, but the overall feel was still unique and creatively inspired.

She laughed to herself as she remembered how important pets, especially little dogs, were in the community. People treated them like full-grown children in Laguna Beach, taking them everywhere. It wasn't unusual to see dogs in grocery store carts or seated right beside an outdoor patio dining table with their own gourmet meals. She thought it was sweet, actually, to see man and canine co-mingle as one society.

Loralee continued to walk down the street, admiring the small business shops and marveling at a few cafés and stores that withstood time. She couldn't resist walking through a secret wrought iron passageway that connected the alley to the main road; and was pleasantly surprised to find a hidden, yet popular gelato shop doling out the goodness to a long line of customers.

She thought it would be worth the wait, and her delectable cup of dulce de leche rewarded her tongue insanely for her patience.

Across the street, she found the opening to the beach and boardwalk, and heard it calling to her. It was much different to approach the warm sand under her toes and smell the ocean up close than it was to peer out over a hotel balcony.

She let her toes dip carefully into the ice-cold water, shuddering at the chills they sent through her unprepared body. Did she remember the ocean ever being this frigid?

Walking along the shore, memories flooded her senses. More family moments with her parents. Beach games with her friends. Quiet time to herself and her journal, pouring her heart out on paper to make the pains of her life swim away. Mistletoe circles and a gentle kiss.

She found herself settling into the sand in a secluded area far from where she first graced the beach. Loralee looked out into the vastness in front of her and simply watched.

She watched the seagulls take flight in the sky, remembering the time that one inched its way over to her dad's lunch box and stole his sandwich.

She watched a sailboat glide slowly along the water and recalled when her friend, Christine, invited her on their family's boat, and they excitedly jumped off the side and swam deep in the ocean.

She watched a lone sea lion playing off in the distance and remembered going to La Jolla Cove every summer to see the spirited creatures swim all around the cliffs.

She watched the waves crash against the side of nearby rocks and transported herself back to colorful tide pools and climbing jagged rocks to get a better view of Catalina Island.

She watched young kids playing basketball off the side of the boardwalk behind her while others surfed the waves in front—some like pros, others wiping out mercilessly with poor timing. She couldn't help but laugh as she revisited the first moments of Evan in his wetsuit with boogie board in hand, determined to ride the ultimate wave.

So much happiness and love resided in these grains of sand and swirls of water.

Why didn't I ever come back when I was old enough? Loralee wondered. *What kept me away?*

Perhaps she had persuaded herself that a life in New York was the only one she knew, and that backtracking would only bring heartache. Now, as she sat upon the welcoming waves of her past, she wasn't so sure she would ever be satisfied with mere cement surroundings.

Oh, how this beach summoned her. How could she ever ignore the connection she had to the sand and water?

After two days of making peace with her past, including a drive-by of her old house and neighborhood to see the vast changes that made it near unrecognizable, Loralee's head was clear and ready to focus on the real reason she was brought back to her childhood home: the opportunity of a lifetime to prove herself as an elite status event planner.

It wasn't often that she battled nerves, but Loralee couldn't help but fidget with her entire outfit as she rose up the elevator to the seventh floor office suite of Brooks Realty. She tugged at her navy blue skirt to straighten it; made sure every single button on her crisp white blouse was done; and measured that her European-style scarf fell proportionately center. Mercifully, there was a small mirror in the elevator that allowed her to fuss with her hair, lip gloss and earrings one final time.

Deep breaths, Ellie. You've got this, she imagined her angelic father telling her as the chime announced her arrival and the anticipation of the open door. *Here goes nothing.*

Loralee walked confidently up to the front desk and was greeted by an overly cheerful receptionist who jumped up at the sight of her.

"You must be Loralee Cox! I'd know you anywhere! I'm so excited you're here," the beautiful young woman with striking red hair and face full of dainty freckles exclaimed. A little embarrassed that she did not recognize the woman, she tried her best to greet her with kind professionalism.

"Good morning," she responded with a friendly smile. "Forgive me, but have we met before?"

"Oh, of course, how silly of me to think you would know me as an adult," she giggled. "It's me, Christine Lucas—well, Donovan now. I'm the one who has been coordinating everything with you these last few weeks."

Joy overtook Loralee as she stood face-to-face with one of her best childhood friends.

"Oh, my goodness, Christy?! I'm so sorry I didn't recognize you. How wonderful to see you!" She forfeited professionalism to take her old friend into an embrace.

"Twenty years and you still are as beautiful as the young girl who left here. What's your secret?" the bubbly worker asked, causing Loralee to laugh and blush at the same time.

"Probably staying single," she winked as if she knew the mystery to youth. Christy just shook her head in admonishment.

"Still as clever-tongued as ever," she giggled. "Come with me. Mr. Brooks is waiting in his office for you. I'll take you to him. When you are finished, what do you say we grab some lunch and catch up?"

"I'd love to. Sounds perfect." Walking into Christy's geniality and familiarity put Loralee instantly at ease. No longer was she nervous to meet the real estate mogul and hope to inspire him with her initial ideas.

"Come on in," greeted the tall, handsome, salt-and-pepper-haired gentleman in a casual green polo shirt and khakis, as if he had just stepped off the golf course. He rose to greet Loralee, extending a firm but gracious hand of welcome as he motioned for her to sit across from his glass desk.

"If you need anything, please let me know," Christy said dutifully as she prepared to exit the office.

"Thanks, Christy. You know, Ms. Cox, it was Christy here who introduced me to your company. You have her to thank for starting this partnership," he admitted with pride for his resourceful employee.

"Really? I had no idea. Thank you, Christy."

"Well, I admit that in doing some preliminary research for Mr. Brooks, I came across your name and instantly had to check to see if you were the girl I knew from old Laguna. When it turned out you were, and I saw the client reviews, I knew immediately that you were the breath of fresh air Mr. Brooks here has been talking about hiring for a few years now.

"I'm just thrilled that I was able to make the introductions. Your work will speak for itself," she winked as she excused herself and left Loralee alone with a very happy executive.

"Indeed, it has already," Brooks agreed. "How was your flight and first few days here?"

"Honestly, long, but I've adjusted well. It was unusual to come back here after so many years, but I've sorted out my personal matters and I'm ready to get down to business, sir. Where would you like me to start?" Loralee asked as she began to dig out the pristine papers from her portfolio.

"First, let's not call me sir," he laughed. "Thatcher will do just fine, and if I may call you Loralee?"

"Of course."

"Excellent. I only have a few minutes today, so I'd love to hear what you've come up with so far, and then I thought I'd bring in some of my staff tomorrow to dig in deeper, as you'll be working more closely with them after this."

"That sounds great," she acknowledged, and then presented a few of her ideas to gauge his reaction. What was refreshing about Brooks was his clear-cut, definitive decision-making process, and she could read what concepts resonated with him and which she should toss.

"I think it's a great start, Loralee. I'm impressed with what I've heard so far. I don't think you've quite captured the overall theme just yet, but I am intrigued by some of the suggestions you have ready to execute once that is set.

"I've got to get going, but I'm sure Christy can help in the brainstorming department. It was nice meeting you," he declared, shaking her hand and walking her out to the office lobby. "I look forward to hearing more of your thoughts tomorrow."

Loralee wasn't sure how to calculate the success of that meeting. He was friendly and communicative, and yet, she thought she sensed disappointment in his tone as the meeting drew to a close. She would have to do additional research to learn more about potential recommendations Thatcher would be interested in before tomorrow.

She sure had her work cut out for her, but was certain that lunch with Christy would be both fun and lucrative.

That it was. They grabbed a table down at a little Mexican-inspired dive along the water, where the old friends exchanged war stories and successes. Loralee regaled her many moving adventures with her mother until Joselyn was ready to settle down, and how she got into the event planning business in the first place.

Christy filled her in on meeting and marrying Theo Donovan, one of their old classmates, and that they had an adorable blonde little 2-year-old boy named Robin.

She happened upon Brooks Realty as a fluke, she said, simply applying for the open position and hitting it off immediately with the big boss. Ten years later, she is still thrilled to be a part of such a prestigious company.

"It sounds like everything turned out amazing for you, Christy. I'm so happy for you," Loralee said with deep sincerity. "And I can't tell you how touched and grateful I am that you found me and recommended me to Brooks. You have no idea how this will change my life."

"Oh, I have an idea," she chuckled mischievously. "But I was happy to do it. Our lives together were cut short as kids, but you were always a wonderful friend to me, Lor. I'll never forget how you were there when my grandma died, and my parents were fighting. I'm happy to return the kindness."

"Well, it was never necessary for you to repay me. But I thank you, nonetheless," she replied, taking a sip of a deliciously spicy margarita.

"My pleasure. So, we've got your work life covered, and you've told me all the gossip with Mama Joselyn and Aimee. What's going on with your love life?"

Loralee almost spit out her drink all over her still-crisp white blouse. "I forgot you pulled no punches," she responded nervously. "Actually, romance hasn't exactly been on my radar for a while. I've been focused on building my business, and I'm happy that way. A man would complicate things right now, so it's for the best."

"If you say so," Christy relented. "I just want to see you happy, Loralee. There is more to life than responsibility, you know."

"If you say so," she teased back, not wanting to explore the topic of her defunct love life and how no man has ever held her interest long enough to be serious. "So, will you be in on this meeting tomorrow?"

"I will indeed," Christy replied, getting the hint that Loralee did not want to probe her romantic status any further. "It will be Mr. Brooks, me and his executive vice president. Don't worry, Lor—you will do great."

"I hope so. I just wish I knew a little bit more about the man so I could come up with some better suggestions. I'm not sure I impressed him that much today."

"I'm sure that's not true. He's an easy man to please, though it is true that he is particular about originality."

"Can you tell me anything about him that might spark an idea?"

"Well…" she began, and as she spoke and lightbulbs illuminated in Loralee's business-savvy mind, the young entrepreneur was grateful to have this comfortable connection that would ground her through the next few weeks.

5

Satisfied that she had just enough new information to formulate a revised proposal for her meeting tomorrow, Loralee departed from her friend to head back to the hotel to get straight to work.

The sun was shining, and it was only about a mile walk back to the Sun and Sands Resort, so Loralee opted for a brisk walk over taking a trolley. She continued to gaze at the nuances of the little town, noting the hand-painted window illustrations, colorful outside décor and lush greenery that surrounded the storefronts—feeling more and more at home with each passing moment.

Realizing she had a long night ahead of her, Loralee welcomed a local coffee shop along the way, where she could stock up on a stronger coffee blend than what her hotel room provided. She noted a single chocolate croissant in the display case and knew it would be the perfect accompaniment for her afternoon caffeine session. All she had to do was settle on the right flavor blend, and she'd be all set.

That was, until a stranger came in and beat her to the line—and to the chocolate croissant. Frustrated, she let out an audible, "of course," and blew out an irritated sigh. The gentleman heard her obvious annoyance and turned around to bravely face the woman to find out what her problem was. Catching a glimpse of his coffee shop nemesis, he chuckled in amusement.

"Well, well, well, if it isn't little miss *that's my luggage,*" Evan chided in recognition.

"You! I should have known it was you who'd be the one taking the last pastry I had my eye on," she huffed back, aggravated that she had to encounter this ill-mannered man twice in one week.

"I'm sorry—I didn't see a red and green ribbon wrapped around it, so I assumed it was free game," he taunted, enjoying getting a higher rise out of his blast from the past. *She's as feisty as ever,* Evan smirked to himself.

"Very funny," she shot back, unamused. "Whatever, go ahead and finish your order so I can pay for my coffee. I have to get back to work."

"Where's the fire, suits?"

"Excuse me? Suits?"

"Yeah, *suits,*" he emphasized. "As in, you New Yorkers are clearly all about business—you know, all suited up for work and no play. Must be exhausting to live that kind of life."

"You don't even know me, surfer boy. I'll have you know I'm not like that." He roared with laughter at her attempt to insult him and her indignation. *Oh, this was going to be fun,* he thought to himself, as she got him just as riled up as he apparently made her.

"Whatever you say, suits. Until later," he mouthed off tritely before walking away with only a black coffee, leaving the coveted delicacy behind, along with a stunned Loralee, who was whisked back to a profound moment in time.

Until later? She reminisced curiously but shook the eerie thought from her mind, refusing to look up at the man just in case—no, he couldn't be. His words were merely a coincidence, just like the rest of the disturbing run-ins with this arrogant jerk. If that were Evan, he would have said something the moment he read her luggage tag.

Sure of her detective skills and dismissal of his alleged identity, she returned to the task at hand to finalize her order and get back to her room to work. She didn't have time for this kind of distracting nonsense.

Suits. Ugh. Loralee had half a mind not to purchase the purposefully left behind croissant just out of spite—but that would only be spiting herself. Lingering in the doorway and waiting for her reaction, Evan chuckled to himself as he looked back to find the sassy siren place her order and take the bait. He knew her well enough to know that pride wouldn't stop her from winning—or from chocolate.

And the way her back straightened and her demeanor froze at the murmur of their special words? Oh, she remembered him all right, but for whatever reason, was either frightened or fighting it—or both. Soon enough, he would reveal himself to her. But not now, not when she was wound tighter than a clock cog. He'd see her again—of that he was sure.

With purchase in hand, Loralee finally turned around to walk toward the exit and out onto the street, pleasantly relieved to find the smug stranger had disappeared. *How irritating,* she fumed in her head. *I hope I never run into that man again. What are the odds that he'd be in Laguna, anyway?*

Loralee spent the rest of the afternoon and late into the evening pining over her updated PowerPoint presentation. Not only did she need to capture Brooks' attention tomorrow, but she also needed to impress another executive vice president—whom she wasn't prepared for.

How much say would this EVP ultimately have? Why didn't Christy give her more information to make sure she would blend both personalities seamlessly? She felt like she was going in blindly, but after six hours of painstakingly outlining a plan she was finally satisfied with, she decided she needed to get some fresh air.

The salty wind soothed her spirit from beyond the balcony. Stars twinkled in the sky, and she could see the three-quarter silhouette of a moon headed toward fullness. There was a stillness in the air that softened her, as she considered the all-too-true analysis of that man in the coffee shop, and the words of wisdom spoken by her old friend.

Her life really was all about responsibility. She rarely made time for friends—and forget about dating. She was too intimidating for men to pursue the likes of her, and she didn't have time to deal with nurturing their masculinity.

No, it was better for her to be on her own, where she could control her comings and goings and not have to get permission from another human to work the hours she did. Her job was her baby—and it was enough for her.

But was it really? she questioned.

Sitting and gazing into the night, she could feel that tug that she experienced every so often when she let herself be vulnerable. After years of being a caregiver and stand-in mother for her little sister, and running a successful business, part of her really did wish there was a gentle soul to come home to at the end of the day. Someone who could help her enjoy life a little bit more outside of her corner office.

But that's not for her to focus on right now. No, right

now, she needed to take a soothing hot shower and get a good night's rest. She would need a lot of energy and mental clarity if she wanted to succeed at winning Brooks—and his associates—over at the meeting tomorrow.

Dressed in a chipper pink and black checkered suit ensemble, Loralee was ready to take on the day ahead of her. She happily greeted her good friend once more as she stepped off the elevator, before being escorted to Brooks' rather spacious, yet sterile, full window office.

As she sat with Christy and waited for Mr. Brooks and his EVP to arrive, she noticed how her surroundings were surprisingly cold; the exact opposite of what the man himself was like. Where he was vibrant, smart and sociable, his office was devoid of any personality.

Sure, his desk was a beautiful, and no doubt expensive, piece of furniture with its glass top and chrome finish. And the few items that decorated his space were valued antiques. But the realtor didn't seem like the kind of man who would care about such material things.

No, she decided, he must have hired someone to set up his office in a professional manner, not taking his character into any consideration. *How dull to have to work under these conditions,* she considered.

His sudden arrival broke her reverie, which, she realized, had been working wonders to calm some of her pre-meeting nerves.

"My apologies for running late," he began, his entrance strong and smooth in stature with the solid confidence of a wealthy man. "I was closing on a deal that took longer than I expected. My associate should be along shortly. He's just escorting our guest out," he explained.

"Not a problem, sir—I mean, Thatcher," Loralee assured him.

"I thank you for taking the time to meet with us again today, Loralee. I know there is not much time left. Did you find Christy to be helpful yesterday?" he asked, smiling with an undoubtful knowingness that his loyal associate delivered.

"Indeed, she was," she responded. "She is a great asset to your company."

"I couldn't agree more," he concurred, their compliments making the humble assistant blush profusely.

"What did I miss?" came the booming voice from the doorway—a voice that paralyzed Loralee before she even turned around.

"Ah, there you are, my boy. Loralee, I'd like you to meet my Executive Vice President, Evan Bosko."

All color drained from her face and all words from her voice. Her palms immediately began to sweat and she quickly looked up at Christy, who nudged her reassuringly with a nod to turn around and meet the grown-up version of her first love.

As she rose with as much class and grace she could muster, all sense of professionalism almost flew out the open window when she realized that Evan and the man from the airport and coffee shop were one in the same. Her mouth gaped open, speechless, but she quickly recovered, knowing that many eyes were watching her.

"Evan," was all she could make out as she weakly extended her hand in greeting.

"Hi, Loralee," he said gently as he took her hand and felt the same rush of electricity she did. He smiled his charming smile, melting away all the meeting mishaps of the last few days. She fought back the tears as she stared into those familiar eyes, and then equally pushed down feelings of anger, as she realized that he knew her all along and never said a word.

What kind of game was he playing? she wondered as she quickly retreated her hand to let him know she was not entertained by his duplicity.

"Do you know each other?" Brooks asked to break the ice, as the tension in the room was undeniable.

"Loralee and I go way back, Pops. She was my first crush," he answered for them, never once taking his eyes off of hers, hoping that she would remove even an inkling of her armor. But she didn't—she couldn't.

"Yes, that was a long time ago. Nice to see you again, Mr. Bosko," she replied, calm and cool, to his—and the room's—disappointment.

"Small world. Evan here is my son-in-law. Well, he was, until Isabella passed," Brooks revealed solemnly.

"I always will be," he responded back with a generous smile, a hint of sadness mixed in with an obvious remembrance of a special girl. It was all so overwhelming for Loralee to absorb, so she defaulted to her normal state of being: businesswoman.

"Will anyone else be joining us today?" she asked.

"No, this is everyone. I wanted Evan and Christy to sit in on this meeting since they will be the ones supporting you in its execution. All they need from me is the sign-off, which I am hoping we can get to today," he said with eagerness before excusing himself to take what looked like an urgent phone call on his cell.

"I'm sorry, but I need to postpone our meeting. An issue has come up on one of the properties I thought we'd be closing on Friday, so I have to attend to this right away."

"Of course, Thatcher. I understand completely."

"Christy, I will need you to join me on this call.

Evan, why don't you stay with Loralee and go through her presentation? You know what I like, and you can help refine anything that might be of interest. And then we can all reconvene tomorrow?"

Alone with Evan? Not even Christy? Her pulse quickened and perspiration started to form under her long wavy hair, which she now wished she had pulled back into her signature bun. Still, she couldn't exactly say no to her newest client, and so, she nodded her head in agreement as her buffers exited the room.

All that remained in Brooks' office was her, Evan and years of unspoken words. Neither knew what to say first, but Evan thought he should start with an apology to break the ice.

"I should have told you it was me when I realized it at the airport. I'm sorry, Loralee."

Sensing his sincerity, she didn't want to be combative, and instead opted for sensibility.

"Why didn't you?"

"I guess I was so rattled at first by your really aggressive attack on me—and then stunned when I saw your name. Plus, you were in such a hurry, I didn't think it was the right moment to spring it on you."

"Okay, I can admit I might have been a little— assertive," she amended. "But then why didn't you say anything when we ran into each other at the coffee shop yesterday? Did you know that you'd be seeing me here today, in this meeting—working on this project together?"

"I did," he confessed, hanging his head. "Look, I don't have a good excuse for my behavior. It was childish of me to keep it a secret and blindside you like this. I wasn't thinking clearly. It's been twenty years, Loralee. I had it all planned out in my head how our reunion would go, and the airport and coffee shop were not part of that vision. It threw me off guard—I'm sorry," he repeated.

Still irked, Loralee could feel her hardened heart soften a bit, believing he was truly remorseful for not disclosing his identity to her sooner. She couldn't quite formulate a response, not knowing how to feel, how to act or how to even look at someone she cared about and missed so deeply that she repressed him into the recesses of her soul.

"It really is good to see you after all this time," he barely whispered, catching what she thought was a runaway tear forming in those turquoise eyes of his.

"It's good to see you, too, Evan," she managed uncomfortably.

"Forgive me for being an ass?" he asked jokingly to ease the friction between them. It worked, because Loralee let out a humorous chuckle, along with a breath of anxious release.

"If you can forgive me for being such a *suit*," she replied, thawing the final thread of hostility that lingered with a wink. Taking her playfulness as a win, Evan decided to play it smart and shift their conversation over to business. He had a feeling that the best way to get Loralee to open up would be to let her do what she did best—use her imagination.

"So, what are some of these plans you have put together for us? Let's see what we can work up for the old goat," he offered.

At ease once again, Loralee confidently delivered some of her best ideas, hoping that one of them would resonate. She'd observe Evan as he considered each suggestion, showing interest but not indicating a clear opinion as transparently as Brooks did. When she was done, she practically begged him for feedback.

"What do you think? Is any of this on target, or am I completely off base?"

"I wouldn't say you are completely off base. I think these are solid suggestions. I just know Thatcher well—he is looking for a 'wow' factor and I'm not sure we've hit it just yet," he said delicately, not wanting to ruffle her feathers or insult her obvious talent.

"What I am missing?" she asked in frustration, sinking down into her chair at her wits' end. She didn't expect planning the extravaganza to be this challenging. She was giving it her all, and was starting to feel depleted to think that her all was not good enough. She scanned the insipid office for a sign of anything personal that could trigger an inspiration of epic proportion.

A mahogany bookshelf with real estate-themed books and a few on golf. Both Brooks and Evan loved the mini golf idea; but of course, it was needing the theme to bring it to life.

A generic crystal paperweight. A bronze Indian totem statue. Canvas wall art of powerful words like Limitless, Grit, Vision and Mindset told the story behind his success, but weren't exactly primed for a holiday interpretation. A glass frame of a pretty young girl caught Loralee's eye, as did a small glass blown figurine of a brown house alongside it. She got up to take in the photograph fully.

The woman had a short blonde bob cut and adorable pixie face. Her blue eyes sparkled and pink lips glistened, radiating a fairy-like quality. Whatever she was doing in that moment brought her great joy.

"Is this Isabella?" she dared to ask.

"Yes," Evan replied with melancholy. "She was the light of his life. One of the lights of mine, too," he admitted with a defeated rawness. "By the time we discovered she had cancer, it had spread from her breasts throughout half her body and we couldn't save her.

"She had such a childlike spirit," he easily shared with deep affection. "When she left us two years ago, she took the joy of the holidays with her. I think that's why it's so difficult to inspire him these days. I don't think he really even wants to have this party, to be honest."

"I'm so sorry for your loss, Evan. And Thatcher's. She sounds like she was an amazing woman. But if he doesn't want to have this party, then why is he going through all of this trouble?"

"He doesn't want to let the community down. It's the highlight of the year. And he knows that any old winter wonderland theme would appease them just fine—*he's* the one looking for some of the joy to come back. If anyone can do it, Ellie, I know it's you."

Just hearing him call her Ellie brought back so many fond memories. She'd gone decades without that nickname and didn't even fight his assumption that it was still okay to call her as such. Whenever Evan said it, there was a tenderness to it that churned unwanted emotions—even more so now that she was a mature woman. She knew that if she didn't keep this to business, she'd be walking down an uncomfortable path of sentiments she wasn't ready to confront.

"Thank you for saying that," she replied meekly with a forced smile. She returned the frame to its coveted spot and took notice of the whimsical little house figurine beside it.

"What's this?" she queried aloud.

"Oh, that's a little gingerbread house Isabella gave him a few Christmases ago. Every year, they would make a gingerbread house from scratch, and make a big mess doing it, too," he laughed. "I wasn't allowed anywhere near the kitchen when they went at it—that was their special tradition."

"You don't say," she replied with a rise of her eyebrows, indicating that her holiday muse had just appeared.

6

"Oh, I saw that light bulb go off. You're not thinking—"

"That's exactly what I'm thinking," she cut him off with an energized glee, grabbing her notepad and a pen to furiously jot down notes. He respectfully held his tongue while he watched Loralee design with abandon, admiring the fire within her that was finally resurfacing; a glimpse of the girl he used to know.

He patiently let her purge her mind for a good half hour, excusing himself to make a quick phone call so she could brainstorm uninterrupted. Though he was certain that even if he remained, there was nothing he could say or do that would break the determined woman's focus.

When he returned, Loralee was chomping at the bit to unveil her brilliant proposal.

"I want to recreate gingerbread magic for Mr. Brooks," she began with an impressive, revised presentation that already had tangible illustrations to match her ideas. Evan was floored by her ability to conceptualize a full vision so quickly.

"First, we decorate the outside of the house as if it were a gingerbread house come to life—but in a classy way. Sprayed snow around the window edges and roof for an icing effect, colorful dangling icicle lights that give the illusion of candy and high-quality candy canes that line the walkway to the front door. Simple, not overdone—but still with a hint of playfulness." She looked to Evan for initial validation, to find him captivated by her enthusiasm.

"Go on," he prodded.

"Once inside, trees are trimmed with assorted gingerbread cookies with white icing and candy pearls. We invite local bakeries to participate in an upscale gingerbread house contest, where all the guests can vote on their favorite display. We can have the bakeries also donate plain cookies, icing and more for guests to decorate themselves—so much easier than having them build a whole house, don't you think?"

"Absolutely. A little childlike but could be fun."

"I know. I get the audience is a little stuffy—but why not give them an opportunity to relax and lighten up; let their inner child out to play? It can still be whimsical but sophisticated. What I am envisioning is not a Hansel and Gretel storybook-style gingerbread. It wouldn't be gaudy—it would be elegant like this beautiful glass blown house right here."

"Yes, that would work. Maybe we can even source a vendor who can make glass blown houses such as these for the centerpieces."

"Oh, I love that idea! It's perfect!" she squealed, adding it instantly to her notes. "And I'm envisioning white lace table linens with gold trimmings, which might complement better than traditional silver this year."

"This sounds really great so far, El."

"Thanks—but I'm not done just yet," she winked while proceeding to her next slide. "How does Thatcher feel about presents?"

"Well, he isn't quite into the grab bag or Santa handing out presents thing, so I'm not sure a dressed up gingerbread man will be his style," he teased as he looked at the slide.

"Yeah, I thought so. Okay. I'll scratch that part. Too family-oriented. I might already be pushing it with the cookie decorating."

"Perhaps, but let's leave the cookie thing on the table and he can cut it if he wants. It surprises me sometimes what appeals to him and what doesn't. He can be quite corny."

"Okay, I will leave that in then," she agreed. "What about holiday swag bags?"

"Yes, that is what we have done the last few years, and it works well. Christy usually takes the lead with those, so I'll let you two work those details out later."

"Great. Then let's keep that tradition intact. Now for music—bands, DJs, carolers?"

"Usually just a band playing instrumental holiday music in the background. It's more of a drink and mingle than a dance event, so we play the music down."

"Okay—I'll need some help in that department since I'm not from around here. Do you think that you can give me the names of some bands I can look into that you've liked in the past?"

"I'll do you one better. I have three that we usually consider for various events throughout the year, so I'll just make some appointments for us to listen to their set over the next week."

"Oh, Evan, that would be so wonderful! Thank you."

"Of course. Is that it?"

"No," she said shyly. "I do want to set up the backyard with a miniature golf station, even if it is only an abridged 5-hole version. We can tie in the gingerbread theme for each hole, and guests can leisurely come out to play in a lit-up garden of white icicle lights. Of course, I'll need to see the space first so I can sketch out how it would all look."

"You are quite the ambitious one, aren't you?" Evan chuckled. "You do realize that you only have three weeks to pull this grand vision off?"

"Are you doubting me, Mr. Bosko?" she asked good-humoredly, challenging him at the same time.

"Not at all. I know once you put your mind to something, there is no stopping you."

"No, there's not," she affirmed emphatically. But I haven't even revealed my grandest plan," she hinted. Loralee then dropped her creative bomb, lulling Evan into a state of speechlessness.

"Again, not doubting you, but given the timeframe, don't you think you are biting off a little bit more than you can chew?"

"Not at all. I admit, it will be a lot of work. But I cleared all my other clients to give one hundred percent to this event. I wouldn't suggest it if I didn't think I could deliver on it. However, I think you are right about one thing—I shouldn't add it into the official plan just yet," she considered smartly. "We can make it a surprise if it all works out, and then if it doesn't, I wouldn't have let Thatcher down."

"I agree, that's a better call. Under promise, over deliver."

"Exactly. But I still want to do it, very much. I will need your help, and Christy's, but I think we can truly make this the best event that Thatcher Brooks has even hosted."

"Is that so?" came the surprised voice as Brooks interrupted the creative duo, with Christy following right behind him. "I take it you've had a productive session while I was away?"

"Yes, Pops, I believe you will be quite pleased with what Ms. Cox has come up with," Evan said on her behalf, making Loralee blush at his adoring confidence in her.

"Well, let's get to it," he motioned, not giving Loralee the chance to let her nerves overtake her. His emergency business was resolved sooner than expected, and he didn't want to wait until the next day when the ideas were so fresh in the dynamic duos' minds in the moment.

And so, Loralee went through the fleshed-out ideas that she and Evan discussed one-by-one, picking up the little glass house to show him the inspiration behind her theme. Her passion and zeal practically moved the gentle rich giant to tears.

"Young lady, it's not very often that someone touches me so deeply. The fact that you came up with this idea to honor my daughter and our tradition has me a bit choked up, if I'm being honest."

"I'm sorry. I didn't mean to overstep or bring up any painful memories, sir—Thatcher," she corrected. "If it's a bad idea that makes you uncomfortable, I can certainly go back to the drawing board."

"Oh no, Loralee, please don't apologize. And don't mistake my emotion for disappointment. I love the idea. Very much so. I clearly made the right choice when I hired you." He paused for a moment, collecting his thoughts, as the room sat quietly in respect of his obvious nostalgia.

"Loralee, I look forward to seeing what you can do with this theme. You have my full blessing to do anything you'd like—including the oddly intriguing cookie decorating idea. There are a few old cronies I'd love to see get some icing on their tuxedos," he joked to break his own emotional tension, raising to shake her hand and those of his team.

"Thank you, Thatcher. I won't let you down," she vowed.

"Indeed, I don't believe you will. Say, what are you doing for Thanksgiving? Veronica and I would love to have you over for dinner."

"Oh—I, um, I don't know. That is so kind of you, but I have so much work to get done, that I really shouldn't take a single day off."

"Nonsense. You have to eat at some point, right? And breaks are good. No one can be productive by working non-stop. Please. We'd be honored to have you. I have other family coming as well, and Evan will be there, so you'll know at least one person."

Loralee tried to fight her cheeks from reddening at the thought of seeing Evan outside of business. She still hadn't processed how they had reconnected after all this time, even though their planning session went incredibly well.

She wasn't sure if she wanted to spend more time than necessary with the man, not knowing how to navigate the swirl of emotions that randomly hit her belly. Still, she knew that it would be ungracious to refuse such a generous offer, and she *did* want to see the inside of that house.

"What can I bring?" she asked with a coerced grin.

With Brooks' authorization granted and an uncomfortable invitation accepted, Loralee was ready to put her plans into action and worry about Thanksgiving another time.

Loralee was grateful for the support she had in Christy, who knew all the right contacts and resources to help her get started. Christy took the lead in getting the swag bags put together and excitedly accompanied her on trips to local retailers for the perfect decorations.

They also worked together to contact a few community bakeries, who were more than happy to promote their business through the gingerbread house contest and cookie decorating supplies. Although it's a busy time of season, none could resist the thought of having their creations on display for the well-to-do to admire and potentially earn new business from.

Loralee even found an entertainment company who specialized in original ideas like the gingerbread-themed mini golf course, and was assured that since money was not an option for Mr. Brooks, she could have whatever she wanted custom-built in enough time to test out before the day of the party.

Evan had kept his word and sourced the perfect artisan to craft the glass centerpieces, as well as arranged for a last-minute meeting with potential bands before the holiday. He organized it in a way that allowed her to tour the house and meet them all at the same time; she was pleasantly surprised by his attention to efficiency.

Though it didn't stop her nerves from acting up at the thought of seeing him again. She had successfully been able to avoid meeting with him in person, resorting to brief follow-up phone calls and texts. He had invited her out to lunch one day, but she tactfully declined, knowing that she had no time to rehash old childhood memories.

If she was going to make this event a success, she needed to focus. Evan Bosko could not be the reason she fell short of her professional promises.

She straightened her chocolate brown dress and added a scarf for just a touch of color. She didn't understand why she purposefully wanted to look dull and boring for Evan, but she imagined if she showed up in one of her more colorful and feminine dresses, he might get the wrong idea about how casual she was willing to be with him.

She still wondered if she should allow him to call her "Ellie" or if she should insist that he refer to her only as Loralee now.

She was overthinking this way too much.

Still, she would send the clear signal that this was business only. She was relieved that he was on the same page, dressed in a black pinstripe suit and tie for the meeting, though she couldn't help but be attracted to this more sophisticated side to the surfer boy she used to know. His eyes sparkled with charm and affection even in his elegance.

"Loralee, this is Mr. Taylor, the groundskeeper. He will be showing us around today before we meet with the bands."

Evan greeted Loralee with the same caution she approached him with. He could tell that Loralee wanted to keep her distance—her refusal to meet him before this was a solid indication of her walls being up, and he was no idiot. He'd have to tread lightly so he wouldn't scare her away. But he wasn't going to back down completely. She came back into his life for a reason, and he wanted answers.

"Pleasure to meet you, Mr. Taylor," she warmly welcomed. "I'm excited to explore this wonderful house."

House? How could I call it a house? she grimaced to herself. It was a massive mini-mansion with four floors of rooms. The bottom floor would be used for the party, with the top three converting into guest rooms for those who drank too much or simply wanted to spend the night in this gloriousness. The hospitality portion of the event, thank goodness, was being managed by another company and not something Loralee had to concern herself with.

As she took in the space, she could picture exactly how it would all lay out. She brought out her sketchbook and got to work—outlining where the trees would stand, where the tables would display the contest houses, where the decorating would happen and where the many food stations would be set up by the caterers for maximum attendee flow and convenience.

She was even overwhelmed with excitement over the backyard space she had to work with, and instantly sent pictures over to the entertainment company to begin their designs. Mr. Taylor also graciously allowed her to invite them to see the yard in person later that very evening. It was more than ample to carry out her golf course and secret idea. She couldn't have asked for a more perfect location to execute her magnanimous concept.

She asked Mr. Taylor many questions, ranging from when they would be able to begin work, to what labor was available to assist with the decorating and set ups. Satisfied to have all her answers, Loralee was ready to move on to phase two of the day to judge musical performances.

While they were waiting for the first band to set up, Loralee fidgeted nervously in her chair alongside Evan, not sure what to say, pretending to be distracted by her phone.

"Great place, isn't it?"

"Oh, yes. It's perfect."

"I can see the wheels turning. I'm guessing you have it all figured out already."

"I do."

"Good. I'm glad it's all working out for you," he

muttered with a hint of aggravation, as she refused to look up and acknowledge him even during their brief conversation. Why was she giving him such a cold shoulder? Didn't they work so well together the other day?

"Ellie, is something wrong?" He felt her back tense at the nickname and questioned if he should even refrain from calling her that as well. What could he do right?

"No, no, of course not. Everything is going so smoothly. I just want to keep it that way," she glanced up quickly with a grin to indicate her all-business mindset. Evan could take the hint, but he also knew he needed to unwind this knot of a woman beside him—just a little.

And he knew exactly how to do that, he thought impishly.

As the first band began to play its melodic festive tunes, he saw the visible change in Loralee from tough to relaxed. Music was second only to the beach when it came to soothing her nerves, and he remembered that much about her. He also remembered how much she loved to dance.

"May I?" he asked as he stood up and reached out his hand.

"Evan, don't be ridiculous. I'm not going to dance to a band audition."

"Loralee Cox, how do you know if the guests will enjoy dancing to this if you yourself do not?" he proposed, making her thoughts churn and her heart beat faster. He had a point, but was this a good idea? The stubborn man in front of her didn't budge, and so, she reluctantly obliged.

How different it felt to be in his arms as a man than when he was a boy. Back then, he was awkwardly thin and not yet changed. Bony and lean. But now? Now he had the arms of a man—one who obviously worked out because she could feel their strength. She could even feel how toned his chest was from underneath his suit. She'd be lying if she said she wasn't affected by his touch.

He was very gentlemanlike, keeping his distance as they swayed to the band, who, she had to admit, was quite good. And he was right—if she could enjoy moving to their symphonies, it would be a good fit for the event. This band had her approval. She almost didn't want to entertain the other two bands that waited to perform; that would mean two more dances with Evan, after all.

Evan, on the other hand, found it difficult to restrain himself from moving in closer to breathe in her floral perfume or from gazing too deeply into her eyes. He had never forgotten what she had meant to him or how much he cared for her—how he still cares for her. He wondered if there was any part of her that felt the same.

Her aloofness could mean one of two things: she felt the same but was scared, or she didn't and genuinely wasn't interested in reliving the past. If only he could figure out which of the two it was.

"Ellie—"

"Don't, Evan," she cut him off before he could even finish his sentence. There was his answer. "Thank you very much," she said to the band, removing herself from Evan's embrace. "We will let you know our decision by the end of this evening. You were wonderful."

Loralee then excused herself to gather up her things, lying about having a conference call in an hour and telling Evan she'd text him her thoughts on who she liked best by the evening. Transparent about her discomfort or not, Loralee needed to make a beeline for the door and out of the presence of Evan Bosko. All he could do was hang his head in defeat as she walked away from a beautiful moment.

What was I thinking? she questioned herself over and over as she drove back to the hotel. Dancing with Evan. How stupid could she be? She reviewed all the reasons why allowing herself to get too close was a bad idea.

They had a childhood connection that should remain in the past. They were two entirely different people now that they were adults. Too much time had passed, and too much guilt over losing touch with him burned her. Besides, she lived on the other side of the country, and he was her client's son-in-law, so what good would rekindling a friendship even do?

And how in the world was she going to survive Thanksgiving dinner?

7

Loralee didn't remember the last time she felt so stressed. She fumbled with her necklace as she debated whether or not to change her dress. She knew this was a personal invitation, and to show up dressed in a suit would be inappropriate.

Yet, she felt unprepared, not knowing what to expect from joining a wealthy man's Thanksgiving table. She didn't even know if the butterscotch pecan pie and apple ginger pear tarts she picked up for dessert were gourmet enough for the crowd.

And let's not forget the fact that Evan would be there, undoubtedly wanting to corner her into a conversation she didn't want to have. She prayed for many interesting guests to be in attendance to absorb all of her attention and give her the diversion she needed.

Speaking of diversions, she did need to video call her mother and sister to wish them a Happy Thanksgiving. She had barely spoken to them since landing in California a week and a half ago.

"Loralee sweetheart, it's so wonderful to see your pretty face," her mother exclaimed. "Happy Thanksgiving, my sweet girl."

"Happy Thanksgiving, everyone," she replied, laughing at the scene of the three men in the background sitting on the couch watching football and shooting her a quick wave hello. Oh, how she adored and missed her brother-in-law and two nephews. She wished she could be sitting there with them or even cleaning up after whatever dinner calamity occurred this year.

"I burned the sweet potatoes and Mom here forgot the gravy," Aimee declared, as if reading her mind. Joselyn just laughed.

"Well, we could all use the cut in calories. Better that then the turkey!"

"What are your plans for today, Lor? Looks like you are all dressed up. Going somewhere?" her sister asked.

"I am. Thatcher Brooks invited me to his home for dinner. I'm really nervous, too. I'm not sure what to expect. I mean, he's a really easygoing guy, but who knows what his relatives will be like."

"Well, they can't be much crazier than us," Joselyn joked. "I'm sure they are just fine. You know, having money doesn't automatically make them jerks."

"Oh, I know. I didn't mean it like that. I just meant, well, it's a different lifestyle and I'm not sure if I'll fit in. I don't even know if I'm bringing the right desserts," she confessed.

"Loralee, just be yourself. A relaxed version of it. Have a glass of wine before you leave to take the edge off and leave the driving to a service. And if it is completely awful, you know how to bow out gracefully. But it may also be absolutely amazing. Be open-minded," her wise sister advised before they wrapped up the call and wistfully left Loralee alone to step outside of her comfort zone.

She decided to have that glass of wine to soothe her final worries, arranging for a car service so she could safely indulge in more wine at the party—and hopefully keep her anxieties at bay.

Two hours, she told herself. She'd stay for two hours to be a gracious guest and then bid adieu to spend the rest of her evening in reflective solitude. There was too much work left to get done for her to take too long of a break, no matter what Brooks advised. But two hours would be enough time to make an appearance and manage discomfort.

Walking into the massive estate, she immediately felt embraced by its cordiality. It wasn't stuffy as she expected—not like Brooks' office. No, it was filled with photos of family, colorful and enticing artwork and vibrant wall colors and curtains. Veronica Brooks cheerfully greeted Loralee as a butler took her coat.

"You must be Loralee. How wonderful to finally meet you. I'm Veronica."

Veronica was every bit as lovely as her daughter Isabella's photo. Small in stature but large in kindness. She had the same fairy-like quality, only bejeweled with dazzling diamonds in her hair and around her neck, filling up the space above her V-neck styled, dark green chiffon dress. Suddenly, Loralee felt underdressed in a simple black cocktail dress and black sandals.

"Come, everyone is in the main dining hall. We don't have as big a crowd as we usually do, so I'm so pleased you are able to join us tonight. We have so much food!"

Veronica skillfully escorted Loralee to the dining area, where she was astonished to see only a few faces there to greet her. She had expected a large family affair with so many people that she wouldn't be able to remember all of their names. Instead, gathered there was only Thatcher, Veronica's sister and brother-in-law, Violet and Thomas Ramsey, their children, Amelia and Bridget, her elder neighbors, Stuart and Gwendolyn Aberdash, and a very handsome Evan—with an open seat next to him intended for her.

Loralee courteously greeted everyone in the room, taking care not to let her eyes linger too long on Evan before taking her place beside him and accepting a rich Cabernet from her gracious hosts.

"You look beautiful," he couldn't resist acknowledging. Tempered by the two glasses of wine in her, she decided that today it would be okay to let her guard down a bit, knowing that by tonight, she could go back to business.

"Thank you. Happy Thanksgiving, Evan," she responded with a genuine smile.

The evening unfolded with unexpected exultation. While it had the appearance of an upscale holiday dinner with violins playing in the background and crystal silverware set before her, the companionship was lively and inviting.

Loralee observed and engaged in the family's charming storytelling of holidays gone by, arguments over who would eat the turkey leg and a round of really awful, amateur jokes. More than two hours had passed, and she had willingly postponed her ride home indefinitely. She couldn't remember the last time she had this much fun.

Dinner was outstanding, and everyone raved over her desserts, which she playfully admitted she wished she could take credit for. Evan watched her with quiet awe as he was able to get to know her better through her lighthearted interactions with strangers as they asked her questions and she answered with ease and confidence.

His heart felt light seeing her so happy—finally seeing the pearly smile that emanated pure joy. How he missed that smile; the one she used to flash at him all the time. If only he could get some time alone with her—there was so much he wanted to say.

"Would anyone care to join me in the library for a brandy?" Brooks asked his guests, full from hours of eating and camaraderie.

"I'd actually like to escort Loralee around the grounds, if that is okay with you?" Evan suggested, to Brooks' approval. On the spot, Loralee couldn't exactly decline the request, and she *did* want to see more of this spectacular home. She smirked at his cleverness to get her alone.

He stood up to pull out her chair and extended his arm to take her elbow in his. *Charming,* she thought to herself. Evan was animated as he took her room by room and explained the history of the place he had called home for the last five years.

He spoke about Isabella and it was evident how much he loved and adored her—how everyone did. Pieces of her existed everywhere here; perhaps that was why this huge house was so enchanting. It wasn't as massive as the mansion they were hosting the party at, but the beachfront property was certainly breathtaking in its own right.

He took her out back for a stroll through the rose garden, its fragrance dazzling her nose and soothing what remained of her nervousness. She had fallen into step with Evan as he guided her through more foliage and out toward the front where the land met the beach. They walked in silence for a few moments until they came upon a rocky area and sat to gaze up at the stars on an incredibly clear night.

"I used to come out here often after Isabella died to just think. I'd imagine she was one of those bright stars and be comforted to know she was still here with me," he confided softly.

"From the way everyone talks of her, it saddens me that I never got to meet such an extraordinary woman. You must have loved her very much."

"I did," he said, pausing, unsure of how to say what he wanted to say next. "I loved her with all my heart. But—she wasn't the only woman I came out here to think about. She wasn't the only one I loved." He looked at her longingly, wishing she would show any sign that his feelings as a boy weren't unfounded.

"Evan—" she started to object and got up off of the cold sand.

"No, Ellie, wait. Please let me talk. Just give me a few minutes of your time and then I won't bother you again," he pleaded, carefully getting up to reach for her hand. She sat back down, unable to refuse his desperate request.

"I just need to know this one thing," he opened, suddenly saddened. "Why did you stop writing me?" The pain washed over both of them at the thought of their lost connection. He with his confusion; she with her guilt. His sorrow was written all over his face and in his eyes, and she knew he deserved an answer.

"We were evicted from our apartment and had one day to pack our things and move," she began. "It was horrible. I quickly threw all my stuff into three different boxes—one being a shoebox of all our letters—and I planned to tell you all about it as soon as we were settled in our new place. But when we got there, I couldn't find that shoebox.

"I can't even begin to tell you how devastated I was that it was gone. I searched and searched but my mom said it must have gotten mixed up with another box or thrown in the trash. I didn't remember your new address and because of the circumstances of the eviction, my mother didn't register a change of address.

"Evan, you need to know I was heartbroken that I couldn't reach you," Loralee professed, the tears streaming down her moonlit-kissed face.

His heart unstiffened at the truth, comforted by the fact that some outside force made it impossible for her to reach him. Knowing that brought him the peace he needed; he was not rejected by his first love.

"I'm so sorry, Evan. I never meant to hurt you like that," she whimpered, trying hard not to let any further cries release.

"It's okay. I understand. Shh," he cooed to solace her, bringing her close into his arms. She allowed it, missing this familiar comfort. Time and space had not changed his ability to draw that silver lining. He took the opportunity to listen more to her stories about growing up in New York, and she returned the favor by asking questions about how life had unfolded for him. Before they knew it, they were old friends again, as if time had never passed.

Shivering at the increasing night's chill, Evan removed his jacket to wrap it around Loralee and suggested that they return to the house before Veronica sent out a search party for them. Not wanting to push his luck with Loralee, he suggested that she return to her hotel for a good night's sleep. Groggily, she agreed, and delivered her goodbyes and gratitude for a wonderful evening.

She was determined now more than ever to bring joy back to Christmas for the Brooks family.

It was back to work for Loralee the second she awoke from a sound slumber on Black Friday. She knew she'd get some great deals and roped Christy into a day of shopping and party planning. Christy didn't mind as much; she was so happy to have her friend back in her life that she didn't mind spending some extra time together.

"How did dinner go last night?" she probed.

"Not too bad, actually. I thought it would be stodgy and uncomfortable, but it was the exact opposite. They really are lovely people."

"I know. I love working for them. You can tell that Thatcher came from good roots and earned his money; it wasn't just given to him. He's a hardworking man with a generous heart. I'm so glad he took a chance on you."

"Thank you again, for that, by the way. This has been such an amazing experience. I owe you one!"

"You don't owe me anything," she reassured her. "But promise me one thing: that when you leave here, we stay in touch. I lost you once and I don't want to lose you again."

"Oh, I promise," Loralee pledged. "After being here again after so many years, it would be hard to walk away from everything I love here."

"Like Evan?" she hinted.

"What? No. I wasn't talking about him," she fumbled over her words of denial. "I was talking about you, and the beach and how I needed to remember how important it was to take time for things that matter."

"Mmm-hmm. You're not fooling me with the 'things that matter.' Why are you so closed up when I ask about Evan?"

"I'm not. That was just a thing when we were kids. Ancient history. I don't know why everyone keeps bringing it up."

"Because it's obvious that whatever you two had is

still there. Loralee, I can see it in your eyes, the way they light up when he walks into the room or after you hang up the phone with him. Why are you fighting so hard against it? Why can't you just let it evolve the way it's supposed to?"

"Christy, I'm here on business. I have a job to do and I can't afford to mess this up. My entire career and future are on the line. I can't get mixed up in some decades-long crush that can ruin my dreams."

"I guess your dreams include being alone for the rest of your life," she suspected, holding her hand up to indicate that she wouldn't pursue the conversation any longer. If her friend wanted to live in denial, then she wasn't going to entertain the idea any longer. "It's okay, I get it. All business. I won't bring it up again."

"Thank you," was all Loralee could reply, as she unskillfully turned the dialogue back toward business and the next steps they had to take to make the event a triumph.

The following week was consumed with preparations and planning. Loralee, of course, had to check in with Caroline, who assured her some events already went off without a hitch and the upcoming ones were in fabulous shape for the same expected turnout. Satisfied with her team's management of affairs at home, she redirected her focus back to the Brooks event and executing every detail flawlessly.

The menus were approved by Brooks and the caterers had their contracted agreement. That lifted a huge weight off of her shoulders, knowing that there was nothing left to do concerning the food until a final count was given two days prior.

The band was selected. The linens were ordered.

The bakeries were busy at work with their confectionary creations and had delivered the marketing pieces needed for the displays. The balloons were ordered. The tables and chairs were rented. The dinnerware was selected.

The entertainment projects were underway and making great time. The crew arrived to begin putting up the lights and converting the front of the house into a gingerbread wonder. Christy was almost done with the swag bags, and Evan confirmed that the artist he hired only had a few centerpieces left to make and then those would be done as well.

All of the pieces were falling into place. Well, on paper they were. Execution was another issue entirely.

She found that she had to supervise the workers to make sure the lights and sprayed snow were hung up in a classy way; they were starting to take liberties with how *they* thought it should look, rather than follow the intricately clear designs she had laid out for them. She could not afford for her vision to come out gaudy, so she went into micromanagement mode.

Then there were the issues she needed to contend with in the dining area, mainly due to her not drawing the room correctly to scale. As a result, the staff had issues arranging the tables exactly how she wanted, causing her to quickly devise a plan to make it work—and ignoring their experienced suggestions in the process. Loralee admitted that her perfectionism could be intolerable, but she would not negotiate when it came to her reputation being on the line.

She also had to keep following up with the outdoor builders, who occasionally got into tiffs with the onsite artist, Beverly, who insisted their golf course structure was not matching her creative vision of the gingerbread décor design for each hole. The constant bickering made Loralee feel like this wasn't going to get done on time like promised—and they hadn't even started on her special project yet.

She went from happily planning to managing a stressful intervention in the matter of a day.

To make matters worse, Evan decided to show up to monitor the progress. She really didn't need this added layer of pressure put upon her.

"What are you doing here?" she snapped at her uninvited intrusion.

"Hey, easy, El. I'm just checking in to see how things were going and if you needed anything." He listened as she turned around to bark orders at the men on the roof and then chased after the golf course adversaries to break up yet another argument. He could see the strain on all of the workers' faces and knew well enough that they were at the end of their rope and ready to quit and walk away if she didn't stop her nagging.

"Loralee, stop," he insisted, taking hold of her arm to grab her attention. "Everyone is about to get up and leave if you don't relax and let them do their jobs."

"But they are doing them all wrong," she insisted. "This is going to be a disaster."

"No, it isn't. They are professionals. They know what they are doing."

"Then why do they keep trying to change the plans? I've given them very specific instructions. I don't understand why they can't follow them."

"Okay, that's it. You have been working nonstop and need to take a break. Sit down right here and be quiet for a moment."

"But I have—"

"It's not a request. As the supervisor in authority, I am ordering you to sit down while I handle the situation." Loralee was speechless and obedient at his command, sinking down into a chair to watch him call together all the workers of the house into a meeting on the front lawn.

"I wanted to thank you all for your hard work. You are doing a great job, and Ms. Cox and I appreciate the quality of your work. That being said, we are going to leave for a little bit and put our faith in you to deliver our expectations. You have been given clear-cut designs and outlines as to how the end result should look.

"When we return, we anticipate that our vision will match exactly what is outlined in your contracts. This event is extremely important to Thatcher Brooks and I am sure if he is impressed with how the details turn out, that there will be bonuses for all involved. We are excited to see what your talents can create."

By the end of Evan's speech, the morale of the workers had shifted from stressed and overworked to positive and inspired, and he was confident that they were grateful to know they'd get a break from the hovering Loralee, who was not so pleased with his bravado.

"Why did you say that? I can't leave right now. I have way too much to do and I'm not sure that I should leave these people to their own devices."

"*These people* know what they are doing and don't need someone second guessing them every minute. And your other work can wait for now. If you don't take a break and cool off, there won't be an event to host. Just do me a favor and trust me, will you?"

"If something goes wrong because I'm not here, I will never forgive you," she pouted.

"Deal. Now, let's go and leave everyone in peace."

"Where are we going?"
"I'm taking you home with me."

8

“Why are we going to the Brooks’ estate? Seriously, Evan, I don’t have time for this.”

“I’m not going to say this again. You need to find a way to relax before you drive us all insane.”

“And how do you plan on doing that?”

“You’ll see,” he smiled, undeterred from his mission to turn the uptight professional into a fun-loving woman again. He led her through the long hallway and into the huge, empty kitchen. She quietly followed, tempted to demand an explanation, but figured it was futile and decided just to play along instead. She knew that look in his eyes—he had a plan and he wasn’t going to stop until he saw it through.

Walking up to the large counter, she could see it lined with all kinds of ingredients. Slabs of gingerbread crackers, bowls of white icing, assorted candies and a beautiful large, empty gold platter.

“What is all this?” she asked, her curiosity finally aroused.

“Well, we can’t exactly have a gingerbread house contest and not have an entry, now can we?”

“Wait, you’re not suggesting—"

“I am. Here’s your apron. Roll up your sleeves and let’s get to creating, Ms. Cox.”

Hesitantly, she put on the festive apron and pulled her

hair back into a neat bun, awaiting further instructions from Evan, who had turned on some Christmas music to get them in the spirit.

"So, what do we do first?" she prompted.

"What do you mean? Haven't you done this before?"

"Nope."

"So, you mean to tell me that you came up with this idea without ever having making a gingerbread house yourself?"

"Hey, I just have the great ideas. Doesn't mean I participate in this nonsense."

"Nonsense? I'll have you know that this is an art form."

"Oh really?" she laughed, softening up her tough exterior.

"Yes. It takes great skill to line up the crackers just so and get them to stand, and then ice it without dripping and placing the candies in the precise spot. Should be right up your alley," he teased.

"Very funny," she replied sarcastically.

Loralee ended up having a much better time than she expected to. It was quite the experience, and Evan was right about it being an art form. Except, she was certainly no artist; oh, she could draw, but that didn't translate to physical sculpting.

There was icing everywhere, and it took a while before they could get the house structure to even stand— completely forgetting that they had to build it on the platter.

Of course, it fell apart in the transfer to the gold plate, which meant they had to start all over again. That started a lighthearted argument, which ended up with icing on Loralee's nose, a gumdrop thrown at Evan's head and then an all-out food fight.

By the time they were done, the kitchen was in shambles and their gingerbread house was a lopsided shack that caught a few misfired candies in its dripping window frames.

"Not sure this would be considered a winner," Loralee laughed heartily at the pathetic structure.

"Well, it might win for originality," he chuckled back. "Come on, we can do better than this." And together, covered in confectionaries, they built and decorated a somewhat decent house for amateurs.

While attempting to admire their artwork, Loralee and Evan stood at the counter noshing on a few broken gingerbread pieces and a steaming cup of hot chocolate with whipped cream.

"I hate to admit it, but that was really fun. Thanks, Evan. I guess I did need a break."

"It was my pleasure. It felt good to just enjoy spending time with you like we used to."

"We did have some good times, didn't we?"

"We sure did. Hey, do you remember that time my mom took us up to Newport Beach and they had the light boat show on the water?"

"Oh yeah! And didn't they have that really small snow area where you could build a fake little snowman?"

"Yup. Now they have an ice slide that people can sled down. It's too bad you're so busy, otherwise I'd take you around some of the latest California holiday traditions."

"I know. I just have so much work to do, Evan. This job is important to me. I need to make sure it is perfect. I can't just go goofing around."

"I understand, Ellie. Really, I do. But life is not always about work. You have to stop and enjoy the moments every once and a while. The Ellie I knew was all about the moment."

"A lot has changed since we were kids. I don't have that luxury of freedom anymore. Do you?"

"I guess not, technically. But I do still make a point to explore the world and spend time with people I care about." He paused, watching her expression of melancholy and strife. From their conversation the other night, he could tell that she had been through an awful lot as a child to make her grow up too quickly, and now she was the master of responsibility and adulthood.

"Loralee, I'm not trying to pressure you. But how about on Wednesday, when things are all set and secure and not much is left to be done, you let me take you out for the day. Just two old friends checking out the holiday adventures around us before we get back to the grind and pull off the best party ever?"

"I don't know, Evan. I just don't think I have the time. I really should be getting back now."

"How about this?" he persisted. "Take a few minutes with me right now to go through everything that is left on the checklist. We'll conference in Christy and see how we can divvy this up between us to take some of the burden off of you. If I could shift some of the responsibility to where you are comfortable, would you consider a Wednesday outing with me?"

"Maybe."

"I'll take a maybe," he beamed, as he dialed Christy's number to get the ball rolling. After only a half hour of going through the details, Evan had delivered on his promise to satisfactorily rearrange tasks so that some pressure was taken off Loralee's plate. Sweetly smug, Evan turned to his friend and motioned that he was waiting for her to have her say.

"Okay, okay," she laughed. "You win. If—and I mean *if*—I am happy with the progress that has been made by Tuesday night, I will indulge your need to take me out on the town. But, if I run into problems, you will have to understand that this becomes the priority. Can you live with that?"

"I certainly can. It's a deal," he agreed, shaking her hand in a mock business-like gesture, causing her to giggle.

"I don't know what I just agreed to," she smiled, shaking her head. "But I do need to return to the house now to check on everything. Thanks again for today. See you tomorrow?"

"Until later," he responded, reigniting her memory of their last moment together as children. She couldn't help but shyly smile and return the sentiment.

"Until later, Evan."

Loralee was a bit disappointed that by Tuesday, there wasn't much left to do. The house had been completely decorated to scale, with only the candy cane walkway to be completed. That would be done by the next day.

The trees were all set up and the staff planned to begin trimming them that evening, since the gingerbread ornaments had just arrived. The centerpieces were delivered a day early, and the tables and inside decorations were also nearly set up.

Even the mini golf course was almost finished; four holes were structurally complete, and the artist was in the middle of painting the third hole's caricatures. All they needed was the fifth hole, which was scheduled to be completed by Thursday. It was cutting it a bit close, but Loralee took Evan's advice and had faith that the workers would deliver.

The band, florist, balloons and caterer had all been confirmed, and no detail had been left unchecked. It was one of the smoothest events she had ever planned, which was surprising considering its complexity and quick turnaround. She beamed with pride as she looked around to see all the pieces fit exactly as she envisioned it.

But that meant Loralee really was free to spend the day with Evan, and she found herself wishing a crisis would pop up so she could excuse herself from her Christmas adventure contract.

She could not go back on her word, however, and decided that she would allow herself to indulge in a single day of festivities without worrying about work. Christy agreed to remain onsite to ease Loralee's tension, and swore an oath that if anything went wrong, she'd let her know immediately.

All dressed up in jeans and a light pink cashmere sweater (even California had its cooler days), she put the finishing touches on her makeup and pulled her curly hair up into a swinging ponytail. Cute but casual, she decided. She didn't want to fuss too much, but it had been a while since she had let herself get ready to enjoy the day with a man.

This wasn't a date, of course, but it made the butterflies visit at the thought of being alone with Evan like this. He refused to tell her where they were going, and although she hated surprises, she knew that whatever he had in store for her wouldn't disappoint.

"You look great," he exclaimed as he met her in the hotel lobby and gave her a quick kiss on the cheek.

"Ready to go?"

"Ready as I'll ever be. And you're still not going to tell me where we are going?"

"Nope. Just sit back and enjoy the ride, Ms. Cox."

After a short ride of easygoing conversation, Evan pulled up to their destination: The OC WinterFest in Costa Mesa. Even though they were in the heart of the golden coast, he wanted to let Loralee experience all the joys of the Christmas season, which meant bringing winter to her.

Her eyes lit up like a child's as she walked through the entrance and onto the huge fairgrounds. There was so much to see, and it all felt so magical—as if she was transported into a fantasyland. She didn't know where to look first; she couldn't remember the last time she felt so swept away by the season.

She felt Evan gently take her hand to guide her toward the festival's Alpine Village, an enormous semi-indoor area where fresh snow was generated daily to recreate a wintry scene with large snowbanks and massive ice-tubing slides. They wasted no time getting in line to race each other down the slides, then jumped right into the cold, wet snow to build a snowman.

An innocent snowball fight broke out, leading them to fall into the soft bank, laughing so hard they grabbed their bellies. Not as familiar with the snow as Loralee was, Evan was taught how to make the perfect snow angel, which was followed up by a warm cup of cocoa and marshmallows.

The day of fun continued on, first with a few candy cane carnival rides and games, browsing through model train exhibits and dining on holiday fare in an adorable Dickens-inspired village. Afterwards, they walked through the event's brand new 50-foot Christmas tree tunnel, lined with animated lights, before coming upon the ice rink.

Loralee thoroughly relished teasing the usually courageous Evan, who was nervous about putting on a pair of ice skates. Finally, there was something she was braver at than he was, and she coaxed him into joining her with the promise that she wouldn't let go of his hand.

Of course, she couldn't keep that promise, as she sped off expertly onto the ice, leaving him hanging onto the rails. She mercilessly rescued him, and eventually, he was able to do a few laps without assistance—though he did look absolutely adorable when he landed hard on his rear-end a few times.

She couldn't remember a day when she felt more free, more alive. And the day wasn't quite over yet.

As the sun set and the night sky took over, park guests gathered before the large tree to anxiously await its nightly lighting. Comfortably positioned in front of Evan, with his arms casually wrapped around her waist, Loralee felt safe and happy. She even allowed herself to lean back into him, feeling his soothing warmth counteract the cool breezes that chilled her.

The tree lighting was spectacular. Not only did the tree dance with colored lights, but the skies above it lit up with the most wonderful fireworks display just as the staged snow began to fall softly upon their heads and noses. She would have never expected such a New York-style holiday experience in California before and found herself enamored with the entire celebration.

"Are you having a good time, Ellie?"

"I truly am. This has been such an amazing day. I feel like a little kid again."

"Good," he responded, closing his eyes and breathing

her closeness in. "I wanted more than anything to bring you some joy. You give so much to others, I thought you deserved to receive some happiness back." She turned around to face him, her walls completely down and a genuine smile spread across her face.

"Thanks for doing this for me, Evan. It's been one of the best days of my life."

"It's not over yet," he winked, grabbing her hand and leading her toward the Mistletoe Lounge for a holiday cocktail and a walk through the vibrant Festival of Lights tunnel. At ease sitting at the edge of the tunnel sipping her peppermint martini, Loralee reached into her pocket for her phone.

"It's strange how I haven't heard from Christy all day. I would have thought she'd at least text and let me know how things were going."

"I'm sure everything is fine," he said, then looked gravely at his own phone and swallowed hard. Things were not fine—Christy had been texting and calling him for the last three hours. "Um, will you excuse me for a moment?" he asked and swiftly moved away out of earshot so he could call Christy back.

"I just got your messages. What's going on?"

"What's going on? Evan, I have been trying to reach you for hours. Why didn't you pick up?"

"Somehow my ringer fell on silent and I didn't hear it. What happened?"

"It's awful. George, the lead builder for the golf course, fell and broke his wrist, and there is no one to replace him. The owner has the flu, and his assistant doesn't have the skills to finish the fifth hole—and he's also been fighting with Beverly, who insists that she's not available to finish painting the last hole after tomorrow.

It's a disaster!"

"Oh, no," he said, running his frustrated hand through his hair and then over his beard. "What can we do?"

"I don't know, Evan, that's why I called you. I knew I should have called Loralee about this immediately. I should have never promised you I'd leave her alone. This could spoil the entire affair."

"Okay. Let me break it to Loralee, and we'll get right back to the house and come up with a solution."

"I'm sorry, Evan. I hope this doesn't ruin your night."

"Thanks, Christy. I'll see you soon," he relented, knowing full well that what he was about to do was going to destroy everything. Taking a deep breath, he returned to an unsuspecting Loralee's side, looking obviously pained.

"Is everything okay?" she asked, concerned.

"Not really. We have to go. There's been a hiccup with the party."

"A hiccup? What kind of a hiccup?"

"An issue with the golf course. I'll tell you about it in the car."

"Hold up," she insisted, grabbing him by the arm and not moving an inch herself. "Why don't I know anything about this, Evan?"

"I told Christy not to bother you today," he answered sheepishly, knowing her wrath was imminent. "I made her swear to leave you in peace and to contact me in an emergency. Just—something happened to my phone and the ringer turned off, so I didn't get her messages until now."

"Please tell me you're kidding! How dare you make that kind of decision for me. This is *my* event; *my* reputation on the line. Do you know what this could do to my business; my life?" she screamed low enough not to draw attention to herself, but firm enough to show her enormous irritation.

"Let's go. I want to know every last detail," she demanded, storming off toward the exit, leaving a frazzled Evan in her wake. He knew he screwed up big time. How could he ever make it up to her?

After filling her in on all that had happened, Loralee immediately conferenced in Christy for another recap and then went to work calling the entertainment company to try to come up with a solution. Using her business savvy and negotiation skills, she was able to convince the owner to come onsite to finish the job himself at the risk of a bad review for a job poorly done.

When all seemed settled and her crisis averted, Loralee felt the anger return and forced herself to stare out of the window for the rest of the drive home. She couldn't bear to look at Evan, who could have cost her everything. She had words for Christy, too, for going along with his foolish plan. Evan didn't dare try to speak until he arrived outside of her hotel to drop her off.

"Ellie, I'm sorry. I should have never put Christy in that position or endangered the party like that."

"No, you shouldn't have," she responded icily, finally turning to glare dagger eyes at his. "And don't ever call me Ellie again. It's Loralee, and you'd do well to remember that, *Mr. Bosko.* We're not little kids anymore, and there isn't some lame mistletoe circle to draw your way out of this one, surfer boy."

Loralee exited the car, slamming the door and walking away before Evan could utter another word. There was nothing he could say to relieve her of the betrayal she felt, or the foolishness of how she carried on like a little girl today while her dreams were falling apart behind the scenes.

A glass of wine and an hour of brooding on her balcony later, she finally let herself get some sleep. There were a lot of reparations she had to make in the morning.

9

It was a long and restless night of sleep—for both Loralee and Evan.

He sat by his ocean view window looking out, regretting how he could have been so careless about something so important to Loralee. He kicked himself numerous times for what had happened, yet wondered, did he deserve the level of anger and hate Loralee spewed at him last night?

Who did she think she was, anyway? *She* was the one who left and lost touch. *She* left him pining away, in love with someone he thought he would never see again in his lifetime. And now that he has, all of those feelings came rushing back, real as day. It wasn't just a youthful crush to him.

But after the way she acted last night, he wondered if he truly was delusional in thinking the woman she grew up to be was the same person that he fell in love with all those years ago.

Up until that bombshell moment, he saw a glimpse of the girl he used to know in the snow-kissed giggles making a snow angel, and in her childlike awe as the sky lit up with wondrous lights. The Ellie he knew. Sorry, the *Loralee* he knew, he corrected himself.

He became bitter recalling her venom and half wanted to leave her to her own devices to figure it all out. After all, isn't that what she's been asking for all along? To be left alone? It was probably best to give her exactly what she wanted.

And yet, he found himself wanting to make it up to her, against his better judgment.

Loralee, on the other hand, was not so generous in her attitude in the morning. She still resented Evan for what he had done and prayed that he had the good sense in him not to come near the event site today. In fact, she wasn't sure she wanted to see him for the rest of the time she was here and told Christy that if she wanted to get back in her good graces, to make sure that Evan steered clear.

Upon arriving at the site, Loralee was pleased to find that more progress had been made on all of the decorations, and that both the front yard and inside were all set for the party, which was only three days away. Nervous to see the conditions that awaited her, Loralee carefully walked out into the backyard to find an almost-finished fifth hole being worked on by the owner as promised.

She walked over to the man with gratitude, thanking him for coming to her rescue in her hour of need and fawning over his beautiful work. She knew after the condescending way she spoke to him last night, he deserved her appreciation and an apology this morning, which she gave freely, and he accepted.

She was even able to convince Beverly to hold out until the evening to finish painting the final piece, which enabled Loralee to finally take a deep breath, step back and realize that all was well again.

"Hey, how's everything going?" Christy meekly asked as she stepped out onto the lawn.

"Better, thanks," Loralee turned with a guilty grin.

"I'm glad it worked out."

"Me too. Listen, Christy, I'm really sorry for the way I acted last night. I shouldn't have gone off on you like that," she apologized.

"No, I deserved it. I should have known better than to listen to Evan. I should have called you the second things went awry."

"I don't blame you. I know how persuasive he can be," she said, looking off into the distance with sadness.

"You know, he was only trying to do something nice for you. He had no idea that something like this would happen. Perhaps you're being a little too hard on him?"

Loralee pondered the wisdom of her kind friend, as she had asked herself the same thing. As irritated as she was with his ludicrous idea to keep her out of the loop, she did know that he never would have purposely put her in a tough position. And she did have a wonderful day with him—a much needed day.

"Maybe you're right. I'm just still so mad at him. He didn't have the right to keep me from something so important."

"No, he didn't. But you don't have the right to hold it against him when it was an honest mistake made from the best intentions." Loralee bowed her head and ran her hand over her face, acknowledging that Christy had a valid point. He deserved an apology just like everyone else did.

"So, what do I do now?"

"Well, he's working from home today. Maybe you should go see him and clear the air. You can't avoid him forever—and you will see him at the party, so might as well get it over with now."

"Thanks, Christy. You are a true friend. Wish me luck," she begged, crossing her fingers that Evan would welcome her apology instead of slamming a door in her face—though she wouldn't blame him if he did.

Loralee knew she couldn't just walk up to the house to see Evan without some kind of remorseful gesture. She remembered how when they were little, the sweet tooth loved chocolate-covered creams and caramels, so she stopped by a See's Candy store to pick up a "forgive me" basket to butter him up.

She rehearsed what she planned to say to him so many times that she feared she'd end up sounding like a robot. She had come to realize that her feelings for Evan were deeper than she cared to admit—to herself or to anyone else.

She didn't want to mess this up; she didn't want an innocent misdeed to ruin the budding friendship they had reignited. She had Evan in her life again, and she was determined to make things right between them.

But when she walked up toward the large, pillared front door of the Brooks home, she heard laughing coming from around the side of the house—one of the laughs belonging to Evan. She was surprised to turn the corner to find him sitting at a small patio table for two, nestled within a quaint little white rose garden.

The woman across from him was a Bohemian-dressed, busty strawberry blonde with waves of curls that had no end. She leaned in toward him in a flirtatious whisper, and whatever she said, made Evan turn and blush profusely. She then placed a small little box on the table, got up to kiss him goodbye on the cheek and sauntered off with an attractive sway that Evan couldn't help but notice and shake his head at with a grand smile.

Loralee's heart sunk, but she couldn't turn away just

yet.

She watched as he looked down at the small trinket-style green box with the fancy gold ribbon and smoothed his fingers over it with an impish grin. Whatever that woman gave him, he seemed to know exactly what was inside and was smitten with his little gift. She suddenly felt awkward for spying on such an intimate moment—and yet, she was glad that she finally witnessed the truth.

Now irate that she had gone through such trouble to apologize to a man who was unmistakably playing her, Loralee backed up behind the porch's lavender bush so the beautiful mistress would not see her as she strolled down the driveway. She then snuck back toward her own car and drove away to the hotel; her chocolate-covered apology package undelivered.

How could she fall for his charm? She should have known that he was only a playboy at heart; that there was no loyalty to an old crush like he led her to believe. She didn't want to admit to herself how hurt she felt at what she just saw—how seeing Evan with another woman hit her soul in a way she never expected it could.

There was a reason she didn't want to open her heart to Evan Bosko—or any man—and this was it. All it caused was heartache and an unnecessary distraction that took her far off task. She had to get her priorities in order. She couldn't let a little misconstrued reunion get in the way of her dreams.

Loralee fought both tears and anger as the traffic-filled road took forever to take her home. Home? A hotel room in an old city was not home. *Home* was in New York—and that was exactly where she decided she needed to be.

Taking advantage of being stuck in traffic, she immediately placed a phone call to Caroline.

"Hey boss, how's it going out in sunny Cali? It's freezing over here! You just missed a few flurries."

"I wouldn't mind a few flurries right now," she responded half-heartedly. "I just wanted to check in on the status of everything."

"Everything has been perfect. We don't have anything this weekend, strangely enough, and all is set for Hetherson, Flinn and Galla next week. It's actually eerily quiet right now!"

"That's perfect, because I need you to do me a big favor."

"Sure, what's up?"

"I need you to fly out to California and take over the Brooks account for me."

"Wait, what? I—I can't do that, Loralee. I wouldn't even know the first thing about managing an event of that magnitude."

"Of course you would," Loralee asserted. "There isn't much left for you to do other than make sure all the line items are taken care of on the day of the party. It will go seamlessly, I promise. And you can call me any time if there is an issue."

"And say I agree to this absurd idea—where will you be?"

"I will be back in New York, and I'll take care of all of our clients left for the year. I can't explain it right now, but I can't be here anymore. I have to leave, but I don't want to risk this account. I need you, Caroline. You are the only one I can trust. Please," she begged. "I promise that once this weekend is over and you come back home, I am giving you the rest of the month off through the new year—paid."

"Oh my, Loralee. Is whatever happened that bad?"

"Yes. Please, I need you to help me. Say you will?"

"Okay," Caroline relented. "I'll do it. Let me just make sure my mother-in-law can watch our dogs, since Tommy will also be out of town on business, and I'll be on the first flight out this evening."

"Thank you so much. I owe you big time."

"Three weeks paid vacation during our busy season is a decent start, that's for sure," she noted. "I assume you are heading out this way tonight as well?"

"That's the plan. I just want to call all of the vendors and alert them of the change in contact, and let Brooks know I have a family emergency."

"Lying to the client. I swear, you owe me a major explanation when I get back."

"I promise, I will fill you in completely. But right now, my priority is making certain that this extravaganza goes off without a hitch. I'll make arrangements for your room here at Sun and Sands and will leave all the files at the front desk, but I'll scan some to you now so that you can view them on the plane and catch up."

"All right. Sounds like you've got yourself a deal. I won't let you down."

"You are about the only person who never has, Caroline. Thank you."

Now that she had successfully convinced her apprentice to step in for her, the more important calls needed to be made. First, to Thatcher Brooks, who fortunately believed her story about having a family emergency and had faith that whoever she sent as her replacement would do a spectacular job if she had Loralee's personal stamp of approval. He also said he knew Evan and Christy had a pulse on the project, so it would be left in good hands, and for her not to worry.

Grateful that conversation went well, she began her line item calls to each company, first to confirm the progress and details, and second, to hand the reigns over to dear, wonderful, life-saving Caroline. Her last call was to Christy, knowing she was currently in a conference meeting and she would get her voicemail.

As far as everyone was concerned, her family needed her back in New York, but that she would be available via phone should anything go wrong.

It didn't take long for Loralee to pack her things, book a hotel reservation for Caroline and a plane ticket for herself. She also decided to leave her little See's Candies surprise up at the desk as an extra "thank you" for Caroline.

She really was doing Loralee a huge favor, though she wasn't sure candy and a mini vacation would be good enough if everything panned out—a bigger promotion would need to be in order. She was aware she was taking a big risk by emotionally reacting and leaving her post, but for her own peace of mind, she had to remove herself from the situation; from Evan.

She ignored the incoming calls from Evan and Christy, who were probably trying to track her down for more information about her "emergency" before she left town. She couldn't wait to be on that plane, where she couldn't be reached by anyone.

As she sat in her snug coach seat, she avoided the garrulous passenger next to her as much as she could by feigning sleep, though she couldn't help but feel the weight of her emotions while her eyes were closed. She was so focused on running as far away from Laguna Beach as possible that she hadn't considered what she was leaving behind. A chance of a lifetime.

A two-hour layover in Las Vegas was the last thing Loralee needed, but it was the best she could do on short notice; though she was appreciative that she was able to get away from Mr. Talkative and prayed that the passengers on her next flight would be much less chatty or interested in her life story.

She briefly turned on her phone to see if Caroline contacted her and found that her associate was already at the airport and about to board her 6-hour direct flight to Los Angeles. But she wasn't the only person trying to reach Loralee. A voicemail from Thatcher Brooks caught her attention, and she knew he was not someone she could blow off.

"Loralee, Thatcher here. I know you said you had a family emergency, but a few issues have come up that require your sole and immediate attention. Please call me back—before landing in New York."

Gulping down her guilt, she hesitantly dialed and prayed for Brooks not to pick up.

"Loralee."

"Thatcher. What can I do for you?"

"Well, you can get on a plane headed back to California. I've given it some thought, and I cannot have my star event planner leaving at such a critical time, even if she swears her associate will do the event justice. I hired you—not your assistant—to personally oversee my event, and I am disappointed that you would pull a bait and switch at the last hour."

"I'm sorry, sir. I just—I need to be back in New York. I assure you that you still have my personal commitment to see this through. I won't drop the ball; you can count on me to deliver on my promises, Thatcher."

"I understand, and I know how important family is.

I would never ask someone to make business a priority over loved ones. However, allow me to ask you this: is your family emergency of such a nature that someone is ill, dying or demanding of your personal assistance?"

"No, sir," she couldn't lie to him any longer, especially when he just called her out for her lack of professionalism. She was already skating on thin ice. "I suppose it can wait."

"Good. Then I expect to see you tomorrow for a breakfast meeting in my office. Safe travels, Loralee."

Loralee hung up the phone and made her way over to the airline counter to change her travel arrangements and hope that her luggage was able to be re-routed in time. She was able to find another flight leaving in an hour for Long Beach, so she didn't have much time to grab a quick bite to eat, call the hotel for her room back and book a car service.

Looks like she wasn't going to be able to avoid Evan, after all. Oh well, she'd have to put her emotions to the side and make amends for almost bailing on her prize contract. She'd pour every last ounce of energy she had into the Brooks Holiday Extravaganza and hopefully repair the damage she already caused with her client's good will.

The question was: what made Brooks change his mind so dramatically after giving her his blessing?

10

“It’s done. She’s on her way back now,” Thatcher announced after hanging up the phone.

“Thank you, Pops.”

“No need to thank me, Evan. I am first and foremost a businessman, and I’m not too pleased that Ms. Cox would let a personal matter interfere with her professionalism. That being said, I do understand how deeply matters of the heart might have affected her on this trip, and I’m willing to overlook this single oversight.”

“I appreciate that, and she will, too,” he said with deep gratitude.

“But Evan—don’t screw it up again,” he said, half-teasing as he gave his son-in-law his blessing to pursue new happiness and love with the likes of Loralee Cox, now that he knew the full story.

After Loralee had left, Evan and Christy figured out what had *really* prompted her to leave. Once Christy admitted that Loralee had gone to apologize to him in person, Evan put two and two together, realizing she must have seen him in the backyard with the centerpiece artist and gotten the wrong idea. Which would have been easy, he confessed, because Anita was a flirtatious young lady and he could just imagine how their interaction would have appeared to an onlooker—especially Loralee.

They then approached Brooks, who intently listened as

Evan revealed their history and all that had transpired up until that point. They deduced that she did not truly have a family emergency, but that it would require a demand from Brooks himself to get her to return to Laguna Beach. All it took was that single, firm phone call, and she had agreed to come back to finish the job.

Evan knew he had to tread lightly—but that he had to do something to show Loralee how much she meant to him. An idea sparked in his mind, and although there were only two days until the big event, he was resolute in doing whatever it took to make it come to pass. He immediately set off to work, and after a few resourceful phone calls, he was pleased that he had figured out exactly how he was going to win Loralee's trust and faith in him back.

The next morning, Loralee surprised Caroline at the door of her hotel room, dressed and ready to head to the office for what would undoubtedly be an uncomfortable meeting with Brooks and team, and she needed Caroline by her side to help her through it.

"Loralee—what? What are you doing here?"

"Change of plans. Come on. You've got a half hour to get dressed before we head into a meeting with Brooks. I'll fill you in on everything that's happened in the car."

Loralee nervously fidgeted with her hair as the elevator rose to the seventh floor; a place she thought she had successfully escaped from and never had to face again. She didn't know how she was going to handle seeing Evan today, but she knew she had to pull it together and get her poker face on.

"It will be okay, Lor. I'm here for you. I have your back. We're going to crush this event," she said cheerfully, giving her friend and boss a much-needed pep talk.

"Hey Loralee," greeted Christy, somewhat standoffish,

yet still friendly. Loralee could sense that her friend was upset with her, and she didn't blame her. She would hopefully take her to lunch or meet her for dinner to fill her in and apologize for leaving so abruptly and deceitfully.

"This is my associate, Caroline Parker. Caroline, this is Christy Donovan—the one who really runs the company," she said in a flattered attempt to make Christy smile. It worked.

"Nice to meet you, Caroline. Mr. Brooks and Mr. Bosko are waiting in the board room. There's coffee, tea and pastries in there. Help yourself, and I will join you in a moment," she motioned while she gathered up her files.

Take a deep breath, Ellie, Loralee imagined her father saying to her. *You've got this.*

She opened the door to a much friendlier welcome than she had expected, and Brooks was pleased that Caroline had joined the team to help with the final preparations. No mention was made about Loralee's attempt to disappear, and it was business as usual as they went through the last-minute details of each portion of the event.

Satisfied that the event was coming together now that Loralee was back at the helm, Brooks excused himself from the meeting and said that he wouldn't see the team again until the big day—and that he was very much looking forward to a special evening that honored his daughter. Loralee could have sworn she saw him wink at Evan as he left the room.

"Well, if that is all, then Caroline and I should get going to check on the progress at the house." Loralee got up to leave, but Evan gently grabbed her by the arm in a gesture to hold her back.

"Loralee, may I have a minute?"

"I'm running late as is it, Evan. Can it wait until later?"

she pleaded with her eyes to let her go; to not make her falter when she had just built her business-focused resolve back up.

"Of course. Let me know if you need any help with anything," he offered dejectedly. He knew that now was not the time to pressure a heavy conversation out of her. Besides, he had some major work to do himself, so perhaps it was best that it waited until his big surprise was ready.

"He's hot," Caroline whispered as they exited into the elevator.

"Oh, be quiet," Loralee hushed, albeit amused with her friend's assessment.

"And he couldn't keep his eyes off you," she pointed out.

"Yeah, well, he seems to have eyes for lots of girls. I wouldn't read too much into it," she said defensively.

"I don't know, Lor. Those weren't flirting eyes to me. There was a lot of love behind those stolen glances."

"Okay, Caroline, enough," Loralee warned. "We have a lot of work to do, and we're not going to spend our time talking about the intentions behind Mr. Bosko's eyes. Understood?"

"Oh, you're no fun," she retorted, enlisting a frustrated chuckle out of the way-too-serious executive.

The last two days went by quickly, without a single mishap and without crossing paths with Evan, which was an added bonus. Having Caroline there to lighten the load ended up being a blessing in disguise—otherwise, she didn't know if she could afford even a nap with all the tasks that had yet to be completed. She was grateful to have her trusted colleague by her side to bring her vision to fruition.

Loralee stepped onto the property with only three hours left until the big reveal; the anticipation of the guests' reaction swirling nerves around her empty stomach.

The decorations inside and out were perfection—including the mini golf course, which exceeded Loralee's every expectation as she played a few practice rounds to ensure it worked properly for the guests. She just knew this would be a big hit and couldn't help but feel pride for fulfilling such a brilliant plan.

The trees were indeed elegantly laced with upscale, circular gingerbread cookies, snow-covered glass ornaments and delicate white twinkling lights. Underneath were piles of trendy swag bags filled with luxury items, such as Coach wallets, 18K gold and diamond snowflake bracelets, high class restaurant gift certificates and other treasures Loralee never dared to dream of purchasing for herself. Christy had outdone herself with the guest gifts.

The glass gingerbread house centerpieces were simply exquisite—and Loralee made the right call to complement them with golden tableware and crystal glasses. She even added the perfect finishing touch by wrapping a wreath of baby's breath around the delicate lace napkins to bring a fresh winter whimsy to the table.

Yes, she thought to herself, this was going to be the most elegant yet playful affair she had ever organized. And she was grateful that Thatcher Brooks warmed back up to her as if she had never tried to leave. She had no doubt that he would love every last detail she had planned for him.

And, she had to admit, she was glad he had called her back so she could see the magnificence for herself.

On the evening of the grand affair, the caterer arrived early to begin setting up the twenty different food stations, from sushi and prime rib carvings to a raw oyster bar and international cheeseboard. Hot hors d'oeuvres were being plated on lace-lined golden platters for waiters to walk among the guests and tantalize their taste buds. A flowing chocolate fountain and mini Viennese table rounded out the desserts. A small sample of a few extras here and there sent Loralee's stomach into heaven.

The acoustics of the band resounded in the halls before the guests arrived, setting the mood for the staff, who were busy at work assisting the caterers, placing fresh flowers in the designated areas and getting the coat room ready for early arrivals.

Even the cookie decorating setup managed to have a chic look to it, if you could believe that. The staff had taken what the bakers provided them and divvied up the ingredients into individual beautiful green mesh bag kits for guests to grab and create. Even the icing was repurposed into an easy-to-use tube and toothpicks were inserted into soft gumdrops.

Loralee couldn't help but laugh at the thought of how "clean" the activity seemed, knowing full well someone was going to accidentally squirt some stickiness onto a very expensive gown.

She then walked into the sitting area, which had been converted into the gingerbread house contest gallery. Three tables lined with unique interpretations of the holiday classic filled the room. She was amazed at the intricacy with which the bakers designed their houses, and with how innovative the themes were.

She wondered how the guests would ever be able to choose a first place winner. One house was made into a barn with trimmings of a southern tradition, which was enchanting. Then there was Santa's house at the North

Pole with silhouettes of hardworking elves in the windows. Someone even modeled the Brooks' estate, which was uncanny in its likeness. On and on the innovation displayed itself.

Another was in the style of a pink princess castle, lined with LED lights that actually worked! That one might have been her favorite—especially since there was a sweet little mistletoe conveniently placed over the prince and princess kissing. She smiled at the charm of it.

As she strolled through the magical exhibitions, she stopped in her tracks and let out a surprised gasp—what was her gingerbread house doing there? It so clearly did not belong among all of the expertly crafted pieces it stood beside.

"I happen to think that's a first prize winner right there," came the familiar voice from behind her. She couldn't help but laugh at the ridiculousness of the idea.

"If it were a contest for 2-year-old gingerbread protégés perhaps," she debated, turning around so she could finally greet Evan face-to-face now that the challenges of the evening were practically behind her.

"This place looks absolutely amazing, Loralee. It's truly the most spectacular Holiday Extravaganza that Brooks has ever hosted. I mean that," he said with the deepest sincerity.

"I hope Brooks feels the same way," she confessed.

"He does," answered the eavesdropping tycoon, coming up to greet the star of the evening. "I must say, Loralee, this is a thousand times better than I ever expected. Thank you for sticking around and seeing it through."

"My pleasure. Did you see the mini golf course out back yet? I think that's my favorite part," she replied.

"I was on my way over there next to hit a few rounds before my buddies take it over. Care to join me?"

"Actually, I wanted to show Loralee something first," Evan replied, then turned to face his teammate. "That is, if you have a few moments before the party starts?"

"I think I can spare a couple of minutes," she offered graciously, realizing that he had her cornered with Brooks watching them and couldn't exactly decline his request. She wasn't too fond of that particular trick of his, but it was effective.

They walked quietly away from the backyard, to an open area off the side of the mansion near the beach. She could see some lights twinkling up ahead, and her curiosity was aroused as they rounded the bend to see a duo of pristine white horses attached to a Santa-type red sleigh.

"What is this?" she asked in surprise.

"It's the gingerbread house tunnel you wanted to create for the party."

"Evan—how—how is that possible?"

"Well, when things went sour that night with the golf course disaster—even though you were acting like a spoiled brat—I wanted to make it up to you somehow. So, I made a few phone calls and worked some magic of my own."

"I can't believe this—it's incredible," she marveled. Out in front of her was the fantasy idea she wanted to surprise Brooks with, but ended up not being able to implement. How relieved she was to have never told him about it, because even *she* came to realize how ambitious of an idea it was.

But here it was, right in front of her eyes. Inspired by Disneyland's annual Haunted Mansion gingerbread display tradition, Loralee had envisioned taking guests on a horse-drawn carriage ride through a magical gingerbread-themed tunnel.

In her vision for an intricate interactive experience, the horse would travel down the enclosed path through an "iced door" opening, and guests would be delighted by scents of fresh gingerbread, dangling lights shaped like gumdrops and a burst of "falling snow" as they exited. It was a daring concept—one that could skyrocket her reputation to the top. And somehow, Evan had made her wildest imagination and hopes a reality.

"I don't know what to say," she whispered, unable to take her eyes off of the masterpiece.

"How about a ride? Shall we test it out?" A huge smile broke out across her face as she took Evan's hand to step up into the carriage for its maiden voyage. She was absolutely dazzled by how flawlessly he took her messy sketched illustration and brought it to life. Every light, every subtle scented spray—even the gentle snow that caressed her nose as their ride drew to a close.

"I don't know how you pulled this off, but—thank you, Evan. I can't believe you did all this. Brooks is going to be thrilled."

"As much as I love to impress the old man, I didn't do it for him. I did it for you," he confessed, taking her hand once again to escort her out of the carriage. She blushed slightly, trying to fight the feelings that he was stirring up inside her. But she couldn't let him get to her, not even with this magnanimous gesture. She still couldn't forget what she saw in the garden and how cozy he seemed with that woman.

"Well, I am truly grateful," she said, looking for some way to get out of the uncomfortable moment. "Can we go grab Thatcher and show him now?"

"I'd like to wait until the party is in full swing, if that is okay," he replied, a little disheartened that she still seemed so reserved. Baby steps, he reminded himself.

"Besides, I know you need to go check your list twice before everyone arrives. I'll take you back up to the house and catch Thatcher on the course for a few puts before he forces me into joining him later. When the moment is right later, we'll escort him outside." Loralee was pleased with that plan and lightened up ever so slightly at his suggestion.

The party went even better than imagined. Guests raved about the food, adored the scenery, danced among the festive trees and even giggled like children as they surprisingly loved making and eating their own cookies. Loralee couldn't have been happier—and neither could Thatcher Brooks.

"I'd say this event was quite a smash hit," he declared, indulging in another sip of his rum-infused eggnog martini.

"You haven't seen anything yet," she said with a wink, then turned to face the attendees. "Attention everyone. There is one more surprise that awaits you outside beyond the garden, if you'll follow me." She locked arms with Thatcher and motioned to Evan, Christy and Caroline to come join them in the lead.

When they arrived at the gingerbread tunnel, she could hear the gasps of awe and excitement all around.

"Loralee, this—how did I not know about this?"

"Truth be told, sir, this was all Evan's doing. You have him to thank for this special addition."

"Actually, Pops, this is Loralee's brainchild. I merely called in the favors to build it. The credit goes to her."

"Well, I shall thank you both. May I?" he asked, gesturing toward the horse like a little boy ready for a grand adventure. "Veronica, my dear, where are you?" Mrs. Brooks hurried on over with glee, ready to accompany her love on a romantic ride through a holiday heaven.

When they returned and other guests lined up for their turn, Thatcher pulled his team to the side.

"Loralee, I cannot begin to thank you for what you have done for us this evening. It's more than just this party, which is rather extraordinary. But you have brought the joy back to Christmas for Veronica and me after losing our daughter, and we never thought that would be possible. For that, we are truly grateful."

"It means the world that I was able to give you both that joy. It was my honor," she replied.

"Now, consider your job done. I want you to take the rest of the evening off and enjoy what you have created," he said, halting her attempt to object with a raise of his hand. "I insist. I have plenty of staff who can see to clean up and break down, and I assume that Miss Caroline here is more than capable of taking care of the vendors?"

"I am, sir," Caroline replied before Loralee could edge a word in.

"Then it's settled. Evan, see to it that this young lady obeys my orders, will you?"

"You got it, Pops," Evan promised, dragging him into a warm embrace as Thatcher whispered "good luck" into his son-by-family's ear.

Loralee wanted to object, but Evan swiftly took hold of her hand and led her down toward the beach for some privacy. But before they could walk any further, Evan stopped them and gestured for Loralee to sit down on a garden bench.

"There's something I need to tell you," he began.

"If it's about your girlfriend, I already know," she responded quietly, wishing that they weren't about to have this conversation. She thought Brooks told her to enjoy her evening—and she was starving, so she preferred to be headed toward the house instead, before all the gourmet delicacies were gone.

"That's just it, Loralee. I know what you saw, but you have it all wrong."

"Do I now?"

"Yes, you stubborn woman, you do. After you took off, Christy told me how you were on your way over to the house to apologize. Oh, don't get mad at her," he said, reading her perturbed face. "She cares about you, and so do I. And I'm glad she told me. It didn't take me long to figure out that you must have seen me in the garden with Anita."

"You're right, I did. And you both seemed quite cozy."

"No, what you saw was our centerpiece maker giving me a special gift I had ordered. She did get a little flirty as she handed it to me—teasing me that if the woman I made this for didn't appreciate it, that she would be more than happy to take her place."

"I bet," Loralee murmured with jealousy.

"The thing is, she could flirt all she wanted, but she could never be the woman that's in my heart." Out of his pocket, he pulled the beautifully wrapped gift box with the gold ribbon she had seen Anita give him. "This was not from, nor for her, Loralee. It was for *you*."

"For me?" She was taken aback by the idea that the whole scene she witnesses was actually about her.

"Yes, for you. But before I give it to you, I have one more thing left to show you."

Without saying a word, surprised by all that he had already revealed, Loralee allowed him to take her hand and lead her down to the beach, where the full moon shone bright and the waves crashed against the rocky shore. Amid all the nature stood an isolated area, and within it, a sand-crafted mistletoe circle with shell holly berries; just like the one he made for her the night she left.

Evan brought Loralee inside of the circle, then handed her the gift box.

"Open it," he persuaded.

Inside was a delicate glass blown figurine of a mistletoe enclosed within a circle.

"Oh, Evan, it's stunning," she cried, unable to hold back a few trickles of tears that made their way to the surface. A piece of paper was carefully placed inside the top of the box, and she gasped as she unfolded it to reveal the very picture she drew for him all those years ago—in the last letter she was ever able to send him. The one of her mistletoe in the sand.

"I can't believe you had this all this time!"

"I never forgot you, Ellie," he said cautiously, hoping that she would allow him once again to call her by that precious nickname. When she looked up at him and smiled, he knew that he had finally touched her heart and reached the girl he had loved for over twenty years.

"When I lost you, I lost a piece of myself. Seeing you all these years later only deepened how I felt about you. Yes, we were children, but it was real for me. I love you more today than I ever did as that silly surfer boy you used to know."

"I tried to fight it, but I can't anymore. You have

always been in my heart, too, Evan. I have never loved anyone the way I loved you," she finally admitted, freeing what had been held back in her for so long.

"I don't want anymore 'until laters,' Ellie. I want until forever now. Even if it means giving up my life here and following you to New York. I don't want to live another moment without you by my side."

"Until forever," Loralee proclaimed, reaching up to caress his stubbly beard before wrapping her arms around his neck in longing invitation.

And then, within their sacred midnight mistletoe in the sand, standing at the brink of where the ocean met the sand, Evan bent down to gently kiss the love of his life, bringing their story full circle. This time, instead of saying goodbye, Loralee and Evan would begin their forever.

Other Books by Jenny Dee

The Lost Heritage Trilogy

Call of the Celts
A Tuscan Treasure
The Catalan Key

Autobiographical Memoirs

Butterfly Travels
Butterfly Travels 2

The Cosmic Kids Club Series

Meet the Z Team
Planet Personalities
Stars Live in Houses, Too
Cosmic Kids Astrology
Numerology for Kids

About Jenny Dee

An avid writer since childhood, my career in professional writing anchored my passion and encouraged my dream to become an author—my first book, *Butterfly Travels,* was published in 2014. Five years later, my children joined me in both my physical and literary journeys, and we are delighted to share our family adventures with the world through *Butterfly Travels 2.*

I've never been a "one size fits all" type of girl. I like to connect to all kinds of people and share my stories and experiences in hopes that they touch a life. I don't ever want my inspiration to be limited to a single genre, so it is with a great love for writing that I offer a multitude of styles to strike your fancy, from travel memoirs and children's books to empowered women's literature and romance.

To learn more about me or to subscribe to my publications, you can find me at www.jennydeeauthor.com or simply scan this QR code.

~ Find Yourself in a Character ~